ALLIES

THE PLANET HOME TRILOGY BOOK 2

C.A. GLEASON

Cover art by Darko Tomic

ISBN: 9798730890985

1. WINDMOTHER

The footprints were substantial, deeper than all the others. She was certain he wasn't flabby. His tracks told her so. They were deliberately paced, controlled with strength, skilled with balance, and sturdy with determination. He was likely twice as heavy as any other man on Home and could only have hidden his path by covering each footstep.

But who would or could? And for how long might they keep up the laborious task? Taking the time to cover tracks would put the person in more danger. Intensify it.

His tracks were practically illuminated to her. He seemed to be someone whose path was not meandering but precise. It wasn't him she was after, it was those who were following him—for what reason she did not know—but she would likely have to track the big man's footprints to find them.

The traitors' footprints were fresh from his within days. Either the big man didn't deviate from his path because he didn't know he was being followed, or he was arrogant. Or there had been a confrontation already.

They probably ran across his path by accident, saw something he was carrying of interest, and began trailing him. She would eventually find out the reason. She could track anyone given enough time. But the ways she would find them were not always so obvious. At first.

She scanned for footprints when possible as they were the obvious sign. But they'd already walked too far and long for her to see them clearly. The wind swept them away—except for the big man's—so she wasn't positive about their specific direction.

One reliable constant was that people often didn't know they were being tracked, so they traveled in a straight line. Regardless of slowdowns, once she caught the whiff of a path she locked onto it. She allowed her eyes to blanket the terrain, absorbing familiar and consistent depressions, ones made by feet at a brisk pace.

Hurried feet were often the easiest to follow. They dragged and fussed the dirt. When tracking a fresh trail, there were often scents of the familiar, like the subtle different colors in clouds. The obvious was the scent of a fire, either active, or one gone out. It seemed they were stopping quite consistently, which meant they were in no hurry and didn't know she was tracking them.

Stupid of them not to know.

Did he really believe he could get away with it?

Even if they were unaware, time was not on her side. If she were unable to reach them within a few more days, or remain close enough to stay on their path, they might deviate from the big man, slowing her too. Her reason for tracking them in the first place might not come to fruition. Never mind how her fellow outliers would react if she failed.

How it would be perceived as weakness. Failing was something she never did. If the expedition turned up nothing, they will turn on her. She will be cast down or out and another will rise up to take her place. She could be dead.

Currently, she still held power over those who waited for her next move and because thriving was what mattered—to her, for her, and for those she cared about—she would do her best.

When one of them suddenly began speaking behind her, an accidental attempt at dismantling their temporary invisibility, she craned her neck and gave him a look she'd given others. He knew it to mean she would kill him in his sleep. The power of control over those who followed her was as strong as it ever was. Even with it always on the precipice of collapsing.

What she decided, went. If she decided to cut a throat, it would be allowed. Those who followed her, would protect her while she held the knife. Although she didn't want to kill the man who inadvertently jeopardized their progression, she would if he couldn't control himself, even though there were feelings for him and it was mutual.

They'd been close. But she'd been close to many men and felt for them all. She wouldn't allow bonds to prevent her from doing what needed to be done. Currently, she was allowing her next decision to happen according to her skills. She snapped her head back and dramatically shook it so they understood she needed to begin the whole process over again.

There were quiet groans behind her, and surely looks of annoyance at the man responsible, and also looks from the others expressing the groaners should muzzle themselves. Even though she didn't care as much about her group as she did about the group they were after, specifically for the one she was closest to and cared for the most, she still must consider caring for them.

Because if it came down to a skirmish, and there well might be, they would fight for her. Being who she was, who they believed her to be, they followed. All of it was temporary and as delicate as the hair she burned before leaving to show them she was strengthening her power. She wouldn't go out of her way to cause her protectors harm, but she'd allow them to die.

The next generation was all who mattered.

The first being footprints, she scanned the distance for the next best way to spot a path; the absence of protein plants. Within the quadrants, was where protein plants grew plentiful; some places it was more, depending on the health of the ground and the rainfall, but where they were pulled more, would grow within weeks.

Until then a trail of empty patches was practically a road leading to those who pulled the food. Where she viewed now had been pulled recently. Importantly, and an obvious clue, before they could grow back. It wasn't the big man who'd done it. His pace was too quick. It was his careless pursuers, those who she was after, who she might have to have killed or do the killing herself.

The layers of their direction splayed out and she decided it was enough to get moving again. When she rose up, she sensed the morale behind her lift in them. Because it meant a new destination. Along with her momentum, theirs returned as a gust as quick as the wind pointing their direction.

Stillness was complacency, walking was a feat creating purpose, leading to achievement. Being useful was all those who followed her desired, and she took pleasure in providing that for them. Once she accomplished what she set out to do and got what she needed from those she was after, they could all return home.

Nothing would have changed except for those of the group she was tracking, who needed to die. Someone would have to be punished. Hopefully not all of them.

The big man made her nervous but she didn't know him personally and he wasn't related to her intent. He was likely oblivious, so he probably wouldn't be a threat. Maybe he would listen to reason if a confrontation loomed. She didn't know if the rumors about him were true. If the rumors were facts, it would change how she would handle things altogether.

But it depended on the depth of his involvement. Inhaling deeply, she concentrated on the consistent foot path depressions, scents, and absence of protein plants. People she needed to track—for various reasons—left at least one of those trails, two if she was lucky. Combined, the group she tracked left all three.

It was meant to be.

She was meant to find them.

And confront them.

2. ROYAH

Along the way they'd found an extra backpack. Clean enough—after washing it out in a lake—to put a baby inside. Royah wore it on her front to carry Emma. Holes were cut so Emma's legs could dangle.

Onnin had put his gun away once he realized, as she had, that the stranger didn't seem to be a threat. Quite the opposite really. She still wanted to keep the conversation going. To make sure.

"What was wrong with it?"

"Damaged battery. Bike was practically shot the moment I put a leg over the seat. Just junk. Even though those things can run for hundreds of years. Maybe longer. I shouldn't have bargained with him."

"Who?"

"It doesn't matter. Either of you happen to have a spare battery in those backpacks?"

Royah shook her head. She looked to Onnin who made no motion. "Who were you bargaining with?" she asked again. "We haven't seen anyone else."

"Good. Hopefully he fell down a hole or something. The guy I traded with."

"What did you trade for it?"

"Doesn't matter. I was stupid."

"Well it must have run for a little while?"

"It did. Long enough to quit on me after the swindler disappeared from view."

"It's not your fault."

"Maybe. But I got taken advantage of. Story of my life."

At first she was hopeful that Buddy could fix the scoutbike.

But in order to do so, he'd explained, he practically needed a new one altogether for a functional solar battery. But if someone did, they might as well keep the one running and abandon the old one.

A lot of times, it came down to which bike was preferred based on the frame because scoutbikes practically ran as long as you wanted to ride them. Unless they exploded, which they sometimes did. She learned that from her mom.

Royah felt she had gone east enough to continue the journey on a bike, but now there were more people with her. They couldn't all fit onto one. Especially considering how big Onnin was. He was surely as heavy as he looked. She would have to wait for a better opportunity.

"So what are you doing out here?"

"I could ask you the same thing. You're quite the trio. Don't see groups like yours every day."

Very true. "I asked you first."

"I'm in between homes. Staying away from threats. Travelling. Seeing the sights."

Royah laughed, but Onnin rolled his eyes. Again. She noticed Onnin rolled his eyes at least half a dozen times already, since Buddy first started following them a few miles back.

Buddy seemed disappointed he was forced to leave his newly acquired scoutbike behind but also seemed to appreciate their company. Random outliers walking around the flat was nothing new.

More accurately, Buddy chose to leave the bike behind to walk in the direction they were heading. It wasn't exactly a surprise. Buddy did a better job of masking his attraction to her than other men. But it wasn't the scary kind of attraction.

So she and Onnin were presently—and silently—deciding how far Buddy would accompany them.

Though Onnin wasn't friendly and didn't talk much, hardly at all, he was perfect to have around because he was so suspicious of everyone. His caution was perfect for the type of quest.

She didn't really want to admit it but she was friendlier with

Onnin than she wanted to be in the beginning, was forcing it more than she wanted to, even though it was authentic, and not because he'd shot at her.

Shot in my direction, she remembered.

Royah understood why he had done it, as she held little Emma. Royah's playfulness came from a genuine place but she was speeding up what might have taken longer for her to do naturally, say if she and Onnin lived in the same town and grown up together or something.

She wasn't sure if he felt the same way but wouldn't be surprised. Men and women who liked each other were naturally drawn together, and Onnin seemed to be keen on everything going on around them. His instincts were strong, so no doubt he must sense how she felt about him.

It was the same with Buddy; her forcing a little bit more of what was natural, offering a more intense version of herself. It was selfish but she was allowing Buddy to follow along, because he could be used as a diversion.

Though unspoken, it was probably why Onnin hadn't objected. They would allow Buddy to endanger himself for them. Even though the man could possibly sacrifice himself unwittingly and propel their quest onward, it didn't stop Onnin from being annoyed with him.

When Royah first asked Buddy if he wanted to go along, Onnin made a comment under his breath about someone else following them, which was humorous because there was no one else. Buddy was the first.

Royah wanted to tell Onnin of course they needed someone else, especially someone who claimed to be able to handle a gun, which Buddy already mentioned he was able to do a couple of times.

As she thought about it, confidence with guns was a helpful skill to have, even if only partially true. Onnin's jealousy piqued her curiosity about what she already sensed; Onnin liked her. She couldn't know for sure. Just a feeling.

Maybe it was a small feeling somewhere inside him still growing, and he might not even be able to acknowledge it or know how to talk about it, but there was definitely something between them.

In turn, that validated how Royah felt about him. For her, it felt nice to be around Onnin, and it didn't scare her to be close to him. Instead, doing so made her feel warm and buzzy.

But it was unspoken and complicated and it might never be brought up. He clearly wasn't the type of man who discussed his feelings. And also, was she really in a state to reciprocate feelings for a man enough to be in a relationship?

Deep down she felt that most men were untrustworthy anyway. Except for her dad, when he was alive of course, and a few others in town, boys she liked when she was younger, and all of them gave her some hope.

Even if Buddy lied, all they really needed was someone who could aim in a threatening manner if there was trouble.

Sometimes a show of force was all that was necessary to survive a shootout. It depended on how much an enemy wanted to live. Everything changed if they were willing to die.

Buddy snapped his fingers. "Can he hear?"

"Better than both of us combined. But it takes him a while to warm up to strangers." She glanced at him, but Onnin didn't acknowledge what she said.

Buddy stared up at him. Then he looked at Royah. "You two," glancing at Emma, "three, been together long?"

"Oh we're not together." She noticed Onnin tense. "I meant, we're together, but not—"

"I know what you meant."

Actually, no, you don't.

"You don't mind me asking questions, do you? If you do, I don't mind minding my own business. Honest."

Royah gave a grin, hiding how she typically felt about strange men. She didn't want what happened in her past to make her treat all of them the same, as deep down she feared they were all dangerous.

Which was true, they were, all men *were* dangerous. Some

were predators. But most used their strength to protect.

"Oh, I don't mind. Ask away."

"How old is your baby?"

She considered lying, but what was the point? "She isn't mine, so I don't know."

"She isn't?"

She shook her head.

"Is she his?"

Again she shook her head.

"Then why do you have her?"

Onnin suddenly glared at him and Royah thought maybe he was going to start answering Buddy's questions with his big fists. She would be wise to do the talking. "We found her."

"Found?"

"She was abandoned."

"Abandoned? Seriously?" Buddy looked at Emma. "Poor thing. What's her name?"

"Emma."

"Nice name for a girl. But if you found her, and she isn't yours, how do you know her name?"

Royah was pretty sure she heard Onnin growl. "We named her obviously. Not sure what her real name is. *Keep up,* Buddy."

He laughed. "Of course." Buddy nodded dumbly. "You going to raise her as your own then?"

"We're taking her to the nearest town. It's the plan anyway." Royah glanced down at Emma.

I'd keep you, but you aren't mine.

"We're hoping to find someone who knows her. Somehow. If we don't, and we don't meet proper parents for her, or a safe place for her either...maybe..."

Onnin glanced at Royah but she avoided his gaze. She didn't know what she'd meant exactly. All she knew was that she liked how things were going at the moment. Not having Emma around likely meant not having Onnin around either, and as of right now, she didn't want him to leave.

She'd had feelings for men before, but nothing serious ever

blossomed. Because she didn't allow it. It could be the same as before but now she wanted Onnin around, and also to protect her. It might just be a crush. Time would tell.

But she really enjoyed mothering Emma. The bond happened fast, quicker than she expected or knew was even possible, when before she thought it wouldn't happen at all.

She also suspected it wouldn't be a big deal to hand her over to another woman or someone who knew what to do with a strange baby. Whenever that might take place. As of right now, the thought of doing so felt uncomfortable.

As if Emma were actually hers, which was strange.

Buddy was walking right next to Royah now. "She doesn't cry much?"

"No. She's a good girl. I've kept her fed."

He didn't say anything, which was unusual. He talked nonstop ever since they met, but he went quiet. When she looked over at him, he was staring at her chest.

Buddy looked away, off in the distance, turning red. "I think I can help you. With whatever you're doing and wherever you're going."

"How do you figure?"

Buddy smiled. "Well, I appear to be headed the same direction as you guys. And that direction would be..."

"East."

"Yeah! East. Me too."

Onnin exhaled loudly, and Royah stifled a laugh.

3. ROYAH

"How do we know you aren't just some outlier looking to rob us?"

"I'm not a robber. Rob you? With him around?" Buddy pointed at Onnin. "Not likely. What would I steal anyway? Emma? No thanks. I mean, nothing wrong with babies and all, but I'm not ready for that kind of responsibility."

"Few men are." When he looked embarrassed, she said, "I'm teasing."

"You don't think I'm an outlier, do you?"

"We'll see." She liked Buddy more and more. He reminded her of a younger brother. Even though he might be older than her. "Now it's my turn to ask you a few questions."

"Ask away. Would an outlier robber answer honestly?"

"One who wanted to trick us would."

Buddy scoffed.

"Where are you from?"

"Everywhere really."

"Everywhere isn't a place I've ever heard of. Where were you born?"

"The town I was born in isn't there anymore. It was near Slingtown."

"What happened to it?"

"It burned."

"Oh." Even though their conversation was playful so far, Buddy had tensed. "Where's Slingtown then? It's not on my map."

"It wouldn't be. I *told* you I could help you. It's south of Easto. They usually have scoutbikes there. It will make going wherever you're going, a lot easier. After you reach a town I mean."

"What?"

"You obviously have plans to go somewhere, but Emma wasn't part of the original plan. Am I right?"

"You're perceptive."

"Thanks—"

"But that's our business."

Buddy looked hurt. "Okay."

Acquiring scoutbikes south of Easto would be east enough to make her mom happy, and Royah was definitely tired of walking. Mayah was correct about foot travel though; it had been safe. So far.

She looked back at Onnin who was listening to their every word as he trailed them, protecting the rear. Looking after others was natural to him. He stared back at her and his right eyebrow raised a little.

Whatever you want to do, he seemed to be communicating.

Scoutbikes were a popular way to travel Home, capable of speeds of about 150 mph at full throttle. There must have been a lot of them in use before the war, considering the aftermath of its destruction and how many were left intact.

Everyone who owned a scoutbike, would run it until the solar battery died, or a driver destroyed it somehow, by crashing it or getting it blown up. They were explosive after all. But those solar batteries lasted hundreds of years when maintained.

Young men always did dumb things according to her mom. The first time Royah rode on a scoutbike, before her mom taught her to drive one herself, was on the back of one driven by a boy who liked her. It was one of the first times she got in trouble.

Her mom had warned her that young men were dangerous because they hadn't matured enough to think straight. And she joked, sometimes they never did.

Riding on a scoutbike with a boy had been so much fun that she was anxious to get back on one ever since. Her mom understood that, which was why she taught her to ride. Even with all of the currency Royah possessed, she could probably only afford one scoutbike.

Except there were other ways to get a better deal by bargaining.

"You've been there? To Slingtown?"

"When I was young. A dangerous place. But useful, if you're willing to take the risk. The men who live there are a little wild."

"No women?"

"So I've heard."

"More wild than out here?"

"You look like you can handle yourself though."

"Thanks. You mean because of my friend back there?"

"Sure helps."

Royah directed her words behind her. "See? We need to stick together."

Onnin grunted and sided up to her on her other side, opposite Buddy. She suspected Onnin was acting more stoic than if Buddy hadn't joined them. Onnin wasn't sure about Buddy yet, which made sense because they only recently met. She probably shouldn't be either.

They were all practically strangers, but she felt she was a good judge of character. She sensed she could depend on both of them. Until they proved differently, she would.

"How do you know the walls of Slingtown are still upright?"

"Chatter on the net. It's still there."

"Who should we meet with when we arrive?"

Onnin swung his head toward her. She turned to him, and he raised both eyebrows this time. Then he shrugged. She learned a shrug from Onnin was a positive.

"You're looking for someone in particular."

"What's his name? I'll charm him."

"I don't remember right now. I'll think of it though. But I do remember what they say about him."

"Who's *they*?"

"Those on the net."

"Okay. What do *they* say about him?"

"He's good with a gun."

"Great."

"Most of the time, when chatter on the net is about how good someone is with a gun, it's because that certain someone wants everyone to think so. But it doesn't mean it's true." Buddy cleared his throat. "I mean not me of course. Everything I've told you is the truth."

"Yeah, sure."

Buddy laughed. "All I know is, what is said over the radio seems to have at least some truth in it."

"Hmm." Thoughts of what Royah heard about Onnin flashed through her mind, and sudden uncertainty along with them. "Who is *they* really?"

"Yeah, right. All of us I guess. I won't say what I heard about Onnin. He's talked about a lot. But I already know what they say isn't true. It's kind of a relief."

Buddy meant it as a friendly gesture, but Onnin was unfazed and remained silent. It would likely take a while for Onnin to open up to anybody.

Including Royah.

4. MELVIN

"Which is the dominant lifeform on this planet, human or battery?"

Melvin waited.

Ash said nothing.

The experiment in Orthal happened around the time he developed his obsession. Was it a coincidence? The mystery of the batteries still eluded him.

Agitated with his thoughts, as if his mind were filled with tiny people chopping away with knives and axes and wouldn't stop until the fleshy truth was revealed. He needed to understand.

It was after dissecting corpses to prepare for an eventual surgery on Pal, when he noticed the similarity between dead men and batteries, which was dormant functionality. Both could still be used for purposes after expiration.

But batteries were the key to everything. The crux of understanding purpose. Batteries held meaning, meaning to him, and meaning to Home. Never mind that he seemed to be the only one who understood.

"Batteries are as much a citizen. They've been here as long or longer. Brought along by the colonists but also the military. Both coexist and within them lie the mystery of human beings, I'm sure of it."

His latest curiosity was the manipulation of solar batteries, tampering with them and causing them to release their explosive energy. To see if it could be directed, or redirected, but most importantly, contained.

When punctured deeply enough with a sharp instrument, he could feel the pulse of power escape. He had looked forward to the next puncture ever since. He enjoyed the way the energy pushed against his gloved hands all at once. It made him feel powerful. In control.

"A lot of what I think is a hypothesis, and I know some emergers are disturbed by my work, but what they don't understand is, at times the best way to solve a mystery is to look at it from a neutral perspective. As I imagine the Alien does."

Melvin turned toward his lab partner, but Ash still said nothing. It was what was best about him. He listened. He didn't chatter away until the end of time as everyone else did. Melvin got back to what he was thinking about.

The meaning behind the batteries intrigued him, kept him up awake for the good part of nights, and sometimes even woke him sweaty from a nightmare. He would figure them out eventually. During his many experiments.

Batteries were basic, invented a long time ago on Earth, existed for centuries, and were still being used by humans, yet the latest iterations were dangerous. How could that be? Humans pushed into space but a common battery was explosive?

And not just the ones powering guns and other weapons, but scoutbikes. Reverting behavior happened to human beings throughout history, but it was unusual for it to happen to technology. It was quite the conundrum.

The experiments on batteries were performed inside a small, hard-plastic container. It was a precursor. A much larger one was in possession. To conduct more bigger and more serious experiments. He inserted his hands into thick, protective rubber gloves.

Wondering what the small container was used for before he discovered it was irrelevant. Probably something to do with weapon experimentation because of its durability. Many of his own experiments ended as flames and smoke. Dark smears wiped out later.

Cutting into batteries, reaching the core, and watching the sudden emersion of stored up energy expel through his specially designed glasses was irresistible. It was similar to when someone died right before his eyes.

Watching under a powerful microscope, battery energy reminded him of basic life at a molecular level. It was curious that death and expelled energy were a similar finality. Experiencing both at his hands, scratched an ever present itch somewhere inside him.

Of course, the truth behind batteries was arrogance. That was the only explanation. They were used in the military by soldiers training with weapons. To a soldier, everything was dangerous or could possibly inflict violence. Why would common devices be any different?

It was why batteries were designed to be explosive. He could think more on it later.

He refocused on the task at hand. Arduous, because it meant relying on others, which he despised. The average emerger was clueless about what was required for experimentation.

If they did, if they could somehow understand the depths of his processes, they would do whatever he asked.

"Do you think they'll respond?"

Ash stared, but Melvin read his mind; not likely. Maybe not even today.

Melvin agreed. He closed his eyes and thumbed the hand mic at the same time. "This is Melvin, over."

Nothing. Empty net fought static.

Whenever he really needed something, no one answered, but it seemed when he didn't, they were all on the net talking about nonsense, rumors, gossip, and overall just wasting time. His time especially.

Opening his eyes, he tried blinking away the dryness, then pinched the bridge of his nose. His head already throbbed. Pinching the bridge of his nose helped a little so he placed the mic in his lap and pushed on the sides of his head with both hands.

His impatience often resulted in headaches and the pressure from pinching the bridge of his nose and pushing on the sides of his head, alleviated them somewhat. Until the pressure was no longer there.

The discovery was another successful experiment he conducted when he was a young man. He couldn't keep pressure constant unless he invented something to fit over his head and bridge of his nose, which he considered. But he could live with the pain.

There were so many important things to do and dwelling on frequent headaches the older he got, was not one of them. He swallowed and dropped his hands away from his head, sensing his lab partner's eye sockets boring a hole into him.

"You're so critical. Mind your own business."

What had he been thinking about?

"Ah, yes."

Emergers who were aware of how many listened to the net—who could be dangerous—during their leisure time, didn't deter them. It didn't prevent them from blabbing. When anything happened on Home, which was typically uneventful now that the war was over, it was still gossiped about.

"Hmm. The war was hundreds of years ago, correct?" He didn't wait for Ash to respond. "Yes."

Occasionally, his mind was as foggy as the flat during morning before clearing. The events of the war also plagued his mind. Ever since he was a boy. But he was so thankful to have made discoveries. Finding answers always reduced the intensity of his headaches.

What was curious was after everything he'd done, it was the battery continuing to haunt him. Self-contained mysteries was what they were. He wanted to think more about them later, and after scribbling a reminder, he definitely would.

What went on over the net didn't affect him personally, even though he got the feeling sometimes it was meant to, but it interfered with his work and for once he'd like to get a hold of someone when needed. Not have to wait for action, attempt after attempt after attempt.

He always considered creating another experiment out of the situation. But it would be changing a major annoyance into a positive. Plus he didn't have the energy to do every kind of experiment he could think of. Not anymore.

Pal hardly told those he led anything of importance aside from a few, so none of them knew how vital Melvin's work actually was. Pal was one of the few who comprehended Melvin's work. Enough to pay him to conduct side experiments.

As for the experiments Melvin conducted on his own, no one knew about them but him and Ash. And those he experimented on. They didn't live through it, so his secrets were safe.

He picked the mic off his lap. "This is Melvin, over."

He exhaled as he waited. Calmer now than when he was younger. A lot calmer. It was a forced evolution. Back then, he was deemed important to a few. Not so much now.

Sometimes, he waited hours for a response. He was being ignored. Probably. The young cared only about the young. Every once in a while, he couldn't get a hold of someone until the following day.

It caused his old self to come rushing back and he thought about hurting people the way he used to, and one of those ways was watching them get hurt by others. Setting up experiments, where they were oblivious to what was happening or why.

But he always knew. And he learned.

These days, age was what he held over others. He was one of the oldest emergers on Home, over 100, except he wasn't exactly sure how many years.

He didn't know his birthday and couldn't remember his childhood. In his mind somewhere buried. Likely for protection.

He understood how the mind worked, knew how it was supposed to work, but it was another mystery eluding him, even though his mind was the same as anyone's. To the degree the mechanics were the same.

Except he wasn't interested in finding out why the memories were suppressed. Nor was he interested in rediscovering them. Something traumatic he supposed and if he knew what it was, it might change him. He didn't want that to happen.

Knowing might alter his perspective. His work must go on.

He had been similar to the rest of them at one time, after the suppression of his memories; homeless, desperate, uneducated, and nothing but an ordinary outlier.

But he was always different by being aware of the struggle by being an outlier, where the rest of them embraced the way of life for reasons he would never understand. They didn't want anything more.

Melvin always wanted more. More knowledge. More understanding. More power.

Nothing wrong with being satisfied while having hardly anything. The biggest difference between him and the rest of them was that he wasn't afraid to change aspects of his life that were causing complications. It was because he understood what was temporary.

Most emergers cared about eating, drinking, sleeping, and having sexual intercourse and not always in that order. They weren't smart enough to realize that everyone could have all of it no matter where or how they lived.

They were on a path out of their control, living one day to the next and reacting to whatever was in their path, without a plan. Melvin felt every moment was controllable, and he liked to decide what happened from one second to the next.

He even discovered, he could control the lives of other people by adjusting their direction so they arrived at a different destination entirely. Figuratively speaking, but sometimes even literally.

If only he could get a response by radio, it would be a lot easier to do what must be done for the day.

5. ROYAH

"The reason I didn't run off when I saw him was because I saw you holding Emma. I figure anybody as nice as you and a baby standing with him was good enough for me. But then again, I've been accused of being naïve."

"No, Buddy. You've got good instincts."

"Anyway, I mean the things I heard about you, Onnin. Hearing them for yourself would probably make you angry."

Onnin said nothing. Not always a good sign. Both men were armed. She could sense a fight looming.

"So," Royah thought quickly. "I haven't listened to the net in a while." Better to divert the conversation from Onnin's past. "Who else have *they* been talking about?"

"You ever heard of a scientist?"

"In school."

"This one is some crazy old man. Out there somewhere. Does all kinds of weird experiments on people I don't even want to tell you about. They say he's gone mad."

"Isn't mad and crazy the same thing?"

"Yeah. I meant mad scientist. It's what they call him."

"Is it true?"

"I sure hope not. There's this swordsman in Easto. Stalks the streets at night, kills anybody who crosses him. Gunblasts can't even kill him. Heard of him?"

Royah shook her head. "How does he spend his time during the day?"

"The same. Hunts down bad folks apparently."

"What's the overseer of Easto think?"

"His dad's the overseer. My point is, definitely don't go visiting

Easto for pleasure."

"We won't."

"And then there's this other guy and he might even be worse."

"Another swordsman?"

"No."

"Crazy scientist?"

"No. Well, in a way I suppose."

"Is he a..." Royah almost said cannibal. She cleared her throat. "How is he worse?"

"Power."

"What do you mean?"

"His control over people. I don't hear about him often, but I suspect he runs a lot of the things going on in some of the towns."

"Going on?"

"Yeah. Shady stuff. And if what is said about him is accurate, he runs all of them. All of the towns I mean."

"Every town?"

"Uh-huh. I also suspect that he controls many of the folks who yap on the net."

"Why do you think so?"

"Of all the people I heard of, he's the one I know for sure is real. I saw him once. In one of those towns he supposedly, almost definitely, runs."

"Which town? Close to here?"

Buddy's eyebrows knit together. "Actually, I don't remember its name. I forgot. I've been to so many towns, I don't remember. But what I do recall was the people surrounding him. Powerful ones mixed in with those who didn't even know who he was. But everyone was sure interested in what he was saying."

"Where was this town?"

"Near Easto. Don't know if it's still upright but knowing he ran it, it probably is."

"You remember a name?"

"No, I told you I don't—"

"Not the town, the man."

"Pal. He goes by Pal."

"Pal, huh? Kind of like Buddy."

"Except I'm friendly. Genuinely. But he just pretends to be." It was obvious Buddy was thinking back. He shrugged. "Just my opinion."

"But we already agreed you have good instincts about folks."

"Thanks."

"What was he like? What did he look like?"

Buddy snorted and shook his head. "You women, always thinking about looks." She was about to object, but Buddy held a hand up. "Kidding." He turned serious. "He was young looking but definitely older. Older than he looks. Good genes. Probably one of those people you hear about, who lives hundreds of years."

He eyed her for a long moment, remembering.

"Some might say handsome. Saw lots of women staring. Dark hair and likes to smile a lot to show off his perfect white teeth."

"Really? Hmm."

"It's what stuck with me about him. It was like he used his smile. Used it like a weapon. And he really knew how to talk to people. To keep their attention."

Someone like him might make another worthy ally. "Any idea where Pal is from?"

"I heard east. But the far east, where no one knows what's out there. I also hear he's organizing all the people out there into some kind of army. An army of outliers."

"For what purpose?"

"Why does anyone want an army?"

Perhaps this Pal wouldn't be an ally, but rather an enemy. And encountering an army would surely delay the quest. "You're as bad as one of those old ladies who sit in a rocking chair listening to the net all day long and gossiping."

Buddy grinned. "I used to have a radio. One of the portable ones."

"What happened to it?"

"Got stolen. Miss my radio. Anyway, Pal is often on the net

talking—"

"You sure it's him?"

"It's definitely him. I remember his voice. Like I said, I saw him in a town once and heard him speak. He invites people to meet with him for reasons he doesn't go into over the net, almost like a code."

"Sounds like you're really creeped out by him."

"I am. But there's something else that makes me think he's even more dangerous than anyone realizes."

Buddy was clearly baiting Royah to continue the conversation, and she could have allowed silence to resume, but the conversation was passing the time and she knew Onnin wasn't going to say anything. Not until he started to like Buddy, which wouldn't be anytime soon.

Royah forced interest. "Realizes what?"

Buddy hesitated. "He *goes* by the name Pal." Then he stared at her as if it were devastating news.

"Wow, Buddy. Absolutely terrifying."

Onnin emitted something sounding like a laugh.

"You don't understand. I don't even think I understand why it bothers me so much. But you see, Pal isn't his real name. He goes by Pal to seem friendly. It's another way to get people to do what he wants. Messed up, huh?"

Royah wasn't sure. "How can a name help with or even build an army?"

"Wouldn't you trust a man named Pal?"

"I don't know."

"There's a lot of intimidating names out there—"

"Like what?"

"I don't know. Onnin, for example. Sorry, big guy. Pal sure isn't one of them. Pal sounds like a good man. Somebody who might help you out. I would believe what a guy named Pal said if I didn't know any better. Maybe the reason it bothers me so much is because, everyone's always nicer to me once they know my name."

Buddy might be on to something. "What's his real name?"

"No one knows."

"Someone must."

"No. Nobody. Not one person. The rumor is, he had everyone who knew murdered."

Royah stifled a laugh. "Unlikely. And doesn't make any sense. Sounds like one of the made up stories."

"I don't make up the stories. I heard it."

"Gossip," Onnin said.

Royah spoke up before the two could begin arguing. "What about him? Himself? Certainly Pal knows his own name."

Buddy chuckled. "You got me there."

Then he got serious when he saw Onnin staring at him as they walked, probably hoping he'd be quiet.

She noticed too. "He's not as tough as he looks."

"Well if he's half as tough, he's tougher than anybody I ever met."

Onnin remained silent. Even after the compliment. Buddy was definitely trying to get Onnin to open up, to like him. There was no reason to distrust Buddy so far, and Buddy clearly believed what he had shared with them.

Royah wanted Onnin to feel the same as her. But after giving them each another quick glance, she knew they weren't going to be friends any time soon. Perhaps her desire for camaraderie was unrealistic. And Buddy wasn't the only one who was naïve.

Onnin was attempting to intimidate Buddy by the looks he gave him and a few choice words, and Buddy was doing his best to pretend he wasn't intimidated.

The last time Onnin rolled his eyes at Buddy, Buddy did the same in return. Seemed they didn't have much patience for each other.

"Everyone who's ever dealt with Pal, remembers him is all I'm saying."

Royah rubbed some dirt off Emma's head as she stared up. "You fear him."

"Far more than I do Onnin."

Buddy seemed to be trying to get under Onnin's skin, to get a reaction out of him, but why? Onnin could fold him in half. Men were so strange.

One minute they were trying to be friends, or even being funny, and then the next minute, they were mad at each other. She'd seen it happen all the time while growing up.

But there was something else about men and their behavior that seemed reliable. Once they got into a fight or an argument, they usually became friends afterward, or at least gained each other's respect, enough to steer clear of one another. Unless one killed the other.

"What else makes Pal so scary to you?"

6. ROYAH

"I wouldn't say I'm scared," Buddy said. "More like wary. It's hard to explain. It's the way he controls the net."

"For example?"

"Requests are actually commands. You'd have to hear him yourself. This is just my opinion, you understand. I hope you never are in a situation with him—"

"Buddy."

"What? I'm getting to it. You in a hurry or something?" Buddy peered around at all the dry, barren flat surrounding them. "Basically, he's able to negotiate for whatever he wants in a town by threatening to replace whoever is responsible, if they don't do as he says."

"Like a corrupt overseer?"

"More like a leader who...It's as if he's in charge of *all of them.* All the overseers. Overseers, of the towns he controls, they report to him."

"Which town?"

"Pick one. Well, maybe not all. As far as I know not Northo, Southo, Easto, or Westo. Not yet, but whichever one between the quadrants he chooses."

"Why not the main towns?"

"I'm sure he's getting to them."

Buddy seemed disturbed by his knowledge.

"You sure know a lot about our fellow emergers."

"Those worth knowing about. Honestly, it's to stay alive. Stay ahead, stay alive. It's what my dad told me growing up."

"Sound advice. And some curiosity on your part?"

"Of course. Something to pass the time. Before my radio got

stolen. And before my scoutbike quit on me. Everything's going *so well* for me these days."

Royah laughed, and Buddy grinned at her. "At least, your sense of humor didn't get stolen."

"Nobody's stealing that from me!"

Royah glanced at Onnin, who seemed to be smiling, but upon Buddy's realization of this, it vanished. Then Buddy's face scrunched together. He didn't understand Onnin's disdain for him.

"Anyway. Hopefully, you won't run into him during your travels." Buddy definitely seemed to be keen on their quest. "Until then, I'd be happy to accompany you as long as you'd like."

"We should head to Slingtown."

Royah stole a glance in Onnin's direction but she couldn't read his expression this time. He shrugged slightly. Even he wasn't sure about the plan.

"Yes? And if you're going further than Slingtown?"

"I want to look at the map. Will you hold her?"

"Me?"

"Why not? If you want to accompany us, you'd better get used to having a baby around."

Buddy hesitated. "Uh, sure."

When she lifted Emma out of the front pack and handed her over, Buddy held her up and away from him as if she might bite.

Onnin stopped to wait as Royah pulled the map out of her backpack. She held it out with both hands, so they could all see if they wanted, carefully obscuring AD.

"So," she pointed with her nose. "Slingtown is about here?"

Buddy cradled and then jostled Emma and leaned forward and squinted. With one hand, he pointed farther east on the map. "No, here." Emma's head tilted up and she looked at him. Buddy looked down at her. "Hi."

A shadow fell over them.

Buddy looked up and behind him to see Onnin leaning over to look at the map. "I thought you were a *cloud*."

"Okay," Royah folded up the map and returned it to her backpack. Then she reached for Emma and Buddy gladly handed her over.

Buddy moved out from under Onnin's shadow and they began walking again. "Slingtown isn't the type of place for a woman. Or especially a baby. Or any of us really. As I was hinting at before, you really need to go to a place like that to go somewhere else, right?"

At first Royah decided to say nothing, like her friend Onnin. Maybe if she ignored Buddy's question, he'd drop it.

"But there is a final destination?"

Royah still didn't want to tell him, but she wasn't good at keeping secrets and Buddy already suspected something else was planned. A smile spread across her face.

"I knew it! Where are you going? Come on, you can trust me."

"We'll see." Royah felt a rumble under Emma's bottom. "We have to stop again. I have to change her."

Best way to change the subject too. The men involuntarily stepped away from the eventual smell. Royah suspected she could rely on Buddy, even though she met him only recently, because of the way he looked at her.

She'd seen men look at her that way before. It was usually in an inappropriate or dangerous way. But Buddy liked her. She could tell. And it was innocent. He wouldn't be a threat. Not to her.

When she finished changing Emma, they continued on. Onnin mentioned that he found plenty of diapers, and Royah was getting rather quick at changing her. Her excrement was buried as it was for all of them.

They always made more protein juice whenever they stopped at a lake by soaking plants in water. The diapers were washed using lake water afterward—and after they filled canteens—and by the time they dried, the diapers were ready for use again.

Thinking about Buddy, the true test of whether he would remain with them or not was if Onnin would eventually accept him. The problem was, she didn't know what Onnin was thinking.

They hadn't been alone since Buddy began tagging along. Like an annoying neighbor with a crush, but one whom she liked.

"You were saying?"

An annoying neighbor pestering, until he got his way.

"I don't want to get into the details because it's a secret. But what we're doing is important."

Buddy's eyes widened. "I believe you. And I definitely want to be involved!"

"You don't even know what it is."

"It doesn't matter. Why lie?" He composed himself, trying to hide how eager he was. Then he leaned toward her and whispered. "Did you tell the barbarian?"

Onnin walked in silence—behind them again, protective and watching over them—but Royah knew he was listening. If Buddy wasn't who he claimed to be or if he turned out to be a threat, Onnin wouldn't hesitate to pull his revolver. He hadn't, so it was a good sign.

"You might as well not whisper," she whispered. "He can hear you."

Buddy glanced back at Onnin and whispered at him.

"I can read lips, boy."

Buddy snickered, and Royah laughed. Onnin's voice was so deep. It was a little scary, but also comforting for some reason. It had a melodic cadence, which she found quite attractive.

Onnin was unlike any emerger she ever met. She was glad to see Buddy wasn't afraid of him. Intimidated, obviously, but not afraid. It showed, he sensed that Onnin was good, as she did.

The best two men on Home were with her for the quest. Probably. It was *their* quest now. The reality was Buddy wanted to go along, and Onnin was glad to be headed in any direction. He was obviously nomadic.

"Well, we should all go together. Me and you and Emma, and the lip reader. Plus, I'm a great shot."

"You told us already."

"And I'm even better company."

Royah could sense Onnin rolling his eyes again.

"Plus, it seems like you could use all the help you can get, seeing as you have a baby and all."

"I can handle a baby."

"Of course you can. I didn't—"

"They're not as complicated as you think. As long as they're healthy."

"Right. Makes sense. Obviously I don't have much experience with babies. See, I like this even more now. I get to learn something. How about you, big guy?"

Onnin said nothing.

"You don't have to talk to me. It's fine. But spend enough time around me and you'll think what others do; I'm likable."

Onnin softened enough to be okay with Buddy going along she supposed, and his lack of an objection settled it. Royah would be okay with Buddy going along with them even farther than Slingtown too.

But it didn't hurt to make Buddy believe she was still undecided. She'd yet to witness Buddy in a gunfight, thankfully, but many men on Home had been part of one. Buddy was still alive, so it meant something.

Another gun, someone who was infatuated with her, which he clearly was, could certainly help keep them all safe, unless he became a problem. Buddy seemed harmless as long as he remained just a friend.

"How about it?" Buddy waited. "Or just to Slingtown. Then you can decide if you want me around after we get there."

She already made up her mind, and wanted Buddy to go along all the way to AD, but wanted him to behave himself. It wasn't wise for women to be too comfortable around strange men. "I'm thinking about it."

"Okay." He waited a few seconds. "So?"

She inhaled and exhaled dramatically. "Fine."

Buddy clapped his hands together. "All right! You won't regret it." He turned to Onnin and pointed at him enthusiastically. "You won't either. You'll see. This means a lot. Thank you. I was so bored before you two, three came along."

"Where were you going anyway?"

"I don't even know! Anywhere. This is gonna be great."

Onnin shook his head and exhaled, and Royah laughed.

7. YOHIRO

Word of his justice changed the town overnight. What had been done to the former overseer and his deputies, should have been done sooner. Except, he was the only one willing to take the risk.

Yohiro had insisted his father replace Bloomfeld as the new overseer, convinced him, and the citizens of Easto unanimously agreed that Ito was the best man for the job.

Ito believed that Yohiro's sword influenced their enthusiasm, and insisted others should run against him. But no one would.

Townsfolk were no longer afraid to speak their minds for fear of being arrested or going outside their homes for fear of violence. Numerous people stopped out of their way to visit Ito's General Store And Supplies to confirm by explaining that. And also do some shopping.

Yohiro suggested, Ito no longer run the store and focus on being overseer, but his father wouldn't agree to that. In so many ways, he got across that he could handle both jobs. Ito decided to split his day. The first half at the store, the second half wherever his role as overseer took him.

Yohiro was confident his father could handle all of his responsibilities, but it meant the store was inundated with visitors and not all of them were there to shop. Many had their own agenda, which made Yohiro nervous.

It was often cumbersome, there was a finite amount of room in the store, and Ito would have to ask people to leave if they weren't going to buy anything to make room for those who were actually shopping.

Then his father came up with the idea of setting up tables outside the store during open hours. There, he would visit frequently while Yohiro worked behind the counter, even if it was raining.

Some goods to buy were put on the tables and a way to distract those intent on chatting with the new overseer inside the store.

There really wasn't enough room to socialize, unless they built extra space outside the store, which was discussed briefly, but for obvious reasons the store—and outside it—became a casual hub, a constant buzz of activity and conversation.

Shoppers could buy or trade at the store, but also talk to the overseer for the first half of the day, and it was shocking to know how many people actually lived in Easto. So many had spent time indoors out of fear under Bloomfeld's leadership.

Not anymore. Now they spent time on the streets. Crime didn't return as Bloomfeld warned and the difference in town was a stark contrast to the bloody violence from his reign. Bloomfeld and his deputies were in actuality the root of the corruption, as Yohiro suspected.

Remove the root of the crimes, remove the crime. Yohiro's actions with his sword saw to it. Recent law-breaking was done by acquaintances of the outliers, who formerly ran the town anyway, and surviving deputies were run off.

Yohiro suspected that some still lurked about, but he would be ready for them.

Yohiro—along with his sword—delegated what happened from the day the overseer was killed onward. Owning guns was legal again for those who wanted to own them, or carry them, but there weren't as many guns to discover in the ground of Easto as other towns.

Also, it seemed people were used to being unarmed under overseer Bloomfeld. Since there was hardly any more trouble, there wasn't much reason to carry a gun. Aside from those who deemed it important, but it was their decision.

There was still some danger going on, except it was under control because it was so minimal. The crimes being committed were mostly robberies by outliers in denial that Bloomfeld was dead.

Implementing order was always necessary, no matter how long peace lasted, because there were always desperate emergers. New leadership was as ready for it as ever.

When Yohiro wasn't patrolling the town, investigating skirmishes and mischief that often turned out to be nothing, or questioning newcomers, he spent his time working at his father's store. And sweeping the floor.

No one challenged Yohiro since the day he killed the overseer —a predicament a brief trial decided was self-defense. Modifications happened quickly.

The former overseer's properties were seized, his remaining deputies fled, and Ito's assistants quickly moved into power.

Ito was already an effective leader and that wasn't just Yohiro's opinion; he heard it from others too. He even overheard them talking about it when they weren't aware Yohiro was near them, eavesdropping.

Shadowing was an inherent skill, but he didn't anticipate having much use for it.

Lately, he was a shadow every day, and trained to get better. He could hide in plain sight and when he wanted, he was practically invisible. His short, unassuming stature, natural agility, and instincts aided him.

Ito met with anyone in town who wanted to do so. He shook hands, listened to concerns, held meetings—a team of advisors were also elected, comprised of prominent citizens of Easto, or they had been before Bloomfeld—and they vigorously discussed obstacles blocking progress.

Outside invasion was always a threat. Especially with rumors of someone organizing outliers into a massive army. Dealing with them was something every town might have to do. Especially one thriving as well as Easto.

Ito was genuinely interested in the circumstances of citizens, how they got along, mentally and physically. Whoever needed help would get help, and whoever could help got paid to do it. Word spread throughout town, and Ito selected those he hired or fired.

Overseer was something his father should have been long ago. Ito didn't just impress Yohiro as his father, he impressed him as a man.

Being a leader is what he did best, not forcing people to do things by violence for selfish and greedy reasons as his predecessor did. Violence was beneath him.

His father listened to what was discussed, internalized and comprehended it to the best of his ability, and addressed those with the concerns, how he believed they should be solved.

What separated Ito from other overseers was how he tackled an issue as a team. He was not a dictator. Someone would inevitably argue with him, or disagree with his advice, or want to add a new idea, but Ito always heard them out, regardless of what he thought.

Ito wouldn't hesitate to adapt to new information, ask questions himself so that he understood the subject matter better, or even admit he was wrong. He would then do his best to figure out what was right to appease both sides going forward.

He appreciated opposing views. He thought the best path was somewhere down the middle. Except he also wasn't afraid to put his foot down, which was when Yohiro turned visible to allow his presence to be known.

Even when Ito's proposals were disagreed with, occasionally vehemently, the people respected him enough to at least try to understand his perspective. Still, Yohiro and his sword at the back of wherever a debate was taking place, didn't hinder their considerations.

During a particular town meeting, one of the discrepancies had been the amount of currency Ito would earn.

Ironically, and to Yohiro's amusement, Ito objected to any payment at all, explaining what he earned from the store was plenty. He also cited what Bloomfeld demanded monthly, even before his nefarious deputies stole more, would take years to pay back.

Ito reminded them of the bank robbery when half the currency was stolen. And then Oliver, the banker, disappeared after

Bloomfeld's death and of course, much of what was left of the currency too.

Along with him, Yohiro suspected. If he ever came across Oliver, he would introduce justice by sword.

Ito's advisors gently demanded he accept payment, and Yohiro suspected it was so there wasn't a scenario where they wouldn't be paid either.

Eventually, it was decided the new overseer's salary would be a quarter of what Bloomfeld earned, and everyone, including Ito, were comfortable with the decision.

Another stipulation by Ito was that he only agreed to be overseer, if he was also allowed to continue to run the store. For him, it was doable due to his work ethic, and Ito's work ethic was something Yohiro was grateful had been passed on to him.

Ito took pleasure in work, enjoyed solving problems, resolving issues, but overall he enjoyed staying busy with so much to do. His new role as the leader of town was a perfect addition to his many responsibilities.

Because he was a businessman first and politician second, Ito's main effort was the store—the first half when early risers were interested in shopping—before assuming his duties as overseer for the rest of it. Being so busy all of the time, every day he liked his schedule more and more.

When Ito's attention went to being overseer, one of his assistants took turns running the store for him. But that meant Ito's day often began well before sunrise and ended well after sundown.

It was likely Ito hoped that someone else would be elected overseer and replace him at some point in the future. Then he could resume his job running the store fulltime, which was his first choice.

Ito didn't voice his thoughts on the matter, and although he did voice enjoying busy all of the time, Yohiro sensed it.

His father didn't hate being overseer, but he didn't exactly want the job either. Often, the people who didn't want the job, were best suited for it.

As the days went on, Easto remained peaceful. So much so it could almost be considered monotonous. Boring even.

There were so many more townsfolk out and about now. Hardly anyone was afraid of theft anymore, so there was a lot more currency changing hands.

There were more and more debates about what went on in town, its people becoming more and more comfortable voicing opinions about what was needed or wanted, who would do the work and who wouldn't, and especially how much they would be paid.

Yohiro enjoyed his work at his father's store, but also as his silent guard when Ito went about his overseer duties.

He was aware that the forward momentum and the recent success and safety in town might be temporary. A transitional period. Viewed as a threat to some. There might be an attempt on his father's life.

If there was, Yohiro would be ready.

8. MELVIN

Then again, it was understandable that others couldn't appreciate his accomplishments. How could they? They didn't possess a superior intellect as he did. His introspective capability was beyond any emerger to the point where, in his opinion, he no longer should be considered one of them.

With their miniature prehistoric intelligences, how could they possibly grasp his thought processes?

Even if he were able to capture their attention for long enough to explain, they wouldn't listen, because of what they heard about him. They said he was mad, so there were already preconceived notions.

Some had listened to him a long time ago, but they were few. The highly intelligent, as he was, were few and far between.

In the last few years, hardly anyone took interest in his knowledge; his words swallowed up by where their scoutbikes took them as they—realistically—drove toward an imminent end.

Controlled by what was impossible to control, which was the inherited, flawed program of being human. Even those he experimented on, wouldn't heed his words. They were self-obsessed, not accepting of the knowledge he offered before their deaths.

It would have saved their lives, as they knew it, by understanding. If they embraced what he told them, it would mean acceptance of being part of something more important. But he ceased attempting to explain himself to his experiments long ago.

It occurred to him that they hardly lived long enough to truly understand anyway. By the time they saw Home as he did, they would be as old as he was now.

Then he would be long dead, and since what he longed for was proved to be impossible, the acceptance of his knowledge by his experiments, attempting such generosity was a waste of his time.

It wasn't that he thought he was better than them, even though he was, it was that he was capable of accepting and implementing experimental results.

He'd grown up like them, and struggled like them too. He lived like everyone else before his life lacked stimulation or meaning, and his frustration had been constant, a meandering nothingness. Not knowing where or how to direct his motivations caused him to be murderous.

Instead of living out his life on a collision course with death as they did, something amazing happened; he made a discovery that changed his life.

And with it, he also discovered his true purpose. Reaffirmed what he already suspected all along; he'd always been meant for so much more.

When older, he realized he'd been conducting experiments since an early age. To alleviate his frustrations. His curiosities. Eventually, he discovered ways of incorporating his feelings of uncontrollable violence into his work, filtering it. But he was alone, knowing of his intent.

Explaining it to lesser emergers would be similar to explaining it to a corpse. Ash understood of course, and the other exception might be Pal. But even he might not accept the depth of what Melvin achieved.

"The amazing find of my life, of our lives, and probably on all of Home, was when I discovered this lab. Discovering it evolved everything about me. I'm beyond thankful. If beyond thankful is even possible. Do you think it is?"

Ash stared.

Deep down Melvin knew the lab didn't create who he was. There would have been something else that sparked the growth. And he would have found some other area of expertise to excel in. But it gave him direction as a young man. It stimulated his mind like nothing else.

Because he lived like others for long enough, before making such a change, he understood them, allowing him to convey what he wanted when he absolutely needed to. As if he were still one of them.

It allowed him to function as part of their society. Had he not, his skills at manipulation might not have evolved. Except communicating with ease could hardly be the description of his interactions.

Recently, during the last few decades, he struggled to identify with their plight. He couldn't understand why they hadn't figured out that all they needed to do, was make microscopic changes and avoid what troubled them to improve their lives. But they did not.

In a way, the lives of others were his ultimate experiment. He was aware of them and how they lived, but they didn't know him or his whereabouts. He hoped to live much longer to follow their paths. To live far longer than what anyone has been told they were capable of so far on this plane.

He hoped to live until he was three- or four-hundred years old. There were rumors some emergers lived over two-hundred years. There were rumors Pal was one of them. But he couldn't be certain it was true. He wasn't about to ask him.

There was no record of such a thing, not any he discovered—he was always searching in reality or in mind—and until it was certified by him, the fantasy of living as long would remain a fantasy.

Another reason he balked to help any of them now by allowing them insight into his knowledge, which was his main reasoning, and a certain name they liked to call him.

"I am not insane. Quite the contrary. Far from it. Highly intelligent, actually. But my superior intellect is something they don't understand because no one else is like me. Sorry, us. And lacking perception causes them to resort to being afraid. To distrust is natural, even I, we, understand, but it doesn't mean I cannot categorize them as they truly are. They are barbaric outliers.

Wouldn't you agree?"

Melvin waited for a response from his lab partner; there wasn't, so he scoffed instead. No one ever called him a mad scientist to his face. Just over the net. If anyone did say it in person, they wouldn't live much longer. Their last words would be pleas for help.

There were always plenty of experiments he hadn't gotten around to, if he needed participants. And to convince them, the only thing that was required was to promise wealth. Then it would be the end for them.

It was easy enough to remain anonymous over the net, but it often meant hearing things he didn't want to hear. The name didn't bother him greatly; they were simply young and didn't know what would happen to themselves decades from now.

Their minds would soften much faster than his own. Even though he was older than all of them. He wished everyone respected him as much as he deserved. And also, that respect could be wielded through his fingertips.

The buzz of empty net stopped briefly when he squeezed the mic. "This is Melvin, over."

9. MELVIN

Before coming to the realization that he was wasting his breath, he would try and help the people ignoring him; what began as an experimental template going forward. Being a helpful old man was a terrific role to distract them from who he actually was in his lab.

Impossible for them to know who they were truly dealing with until it was too late.

He tried ignoring his murderous impulses—for years—and suggested they remain in groups to survive by helping one another. The suggestions were obvious, logical, and he would have been able to identify which of them were smart enough to listen.

He was optimistic they would abide by his advice at first, but he wasn't surprised when they abandoned it, or plain forgot, and fled in unplanned directions in an attempt to accomplish the impossible, which was to live a full life.

To survive, they needed to pay strict attention and implement every component of what he instructed them to do. He wasn't disappointed when they didn't abide by his instructions. He found it more curious, but it was all part of an experiment.

He often offered advice during his many experiments, but the real reason was to explore if anyone was similar to himself, and smart enough to understand his thought processes and intentions.

But hardly anyone heeded what he said. They listened to their own flawed instincts and headed far east to search for currency or guns, they somehow believed were conveniently waiting for them.

By exploring, they were just endangering themselves unnecessarily to obtain more of what they already owned. More was just more of the same. It was what flawed most emergers.

A few years ago, many years in fact, there'd been a few who actually took to his teachings. For them Melvin gave shelter, a sense of belonging, and an understanding of existence.

Then he commanded them to scour Home for guns, radios, batteries, or anything else he deemed useful, especially currency. He didn't believe in its power, just its power over others. Much of what they discovered for him, he possessed to this day.

Melvin might be the only one to understand currency was nothing more than an illusion. No real value like his knowledge. Yet for some reason, the perceived value of currency was a concept that infected minds.

His own understanding of greed was rare, and currency not influencing his every move rarer still, because he was not a typical outlier.

The few who adapted his teachings died many years ago. Those he sent out soon never returned. They likely got themselves killed, or perhaps even few of the few defected from his commands.

Back then he was on his own, but now there was Ash as a lab partner. And Melvin also did some work for Pal. Everyone seemed to think Pal was Melvin's boss.

Melvin pretended to be a subordinate because realistically he lacked the power to change minds as Pal did.

Melvin wasn't as persuasive as the man he pretended to work for, but along with the outliers, who lived and looted for Pal, practically following him blindly, gave Melvin a veil of similar power. It allowed him to continue his experiments, which was all he cared about.

Pal, by protecting all he commanded, gave them all purpose, identities, and hope for the future. Many of the outliers would sacrifice everything for Pal and often did. Melvin pretended he would too. This allowed him to control without their knowledge.

Though technically in business with someone other than Ash,

without Pal, all of Melvin's newly established power would likely vanish. Then he would once again be on his own. Doable, but not ideal.

"I know what you're thinking but you're wrong. My understanding makes it so, I respect and appreciate all I have and have obtained, but I'm waiting to capitalize on any error by him and take over."

There was a flutter in his stomach, the same way he felt when energy hit his gloved hands, or when a life ended right before his eyes.

"You know what I mean to do. You hear me? Even though I respect him. Except he's too smart to fall for any ordinary plot. He too shows respect for those who follow his orders but he's also perceptive, cautious, and secretively paranoid. As are we. More so. It's one of the characteristics we have in common. We're aware but we pretend we are not. It's amusing, don't you think?"

Melvin shrugged at Ash's silence. It was a rhetorical question anyway, as all questions ended up being, when involving his lab partner.

Some who followed Pal, an unfortunate few, tried to overthrow him recently but it was brief. He destroyed them, but the botched coup lasted long enough for word to spread of what Pal truly was. Dictator fit well. His friendliness a mask, one he used to hide his true self.

Melvin recognized the trait, for it was one he possessed too. A strength simmering beneath the surface but hidden well. Most believed him to be a friendly. Just a helpful old man.

Melvin was fortunate that he never was accosted by Pal's true self, to have it come forth the way he was feared, which was the way he was described behind his back in whispers, or known by those he defeated.

Melvin and Pal were in business together, so being combative never occurred. And also, Melvin recognized Pal's unmistakable strength. It was in his eyes, under the surface of his actions, but always ready to arise.

Pal was observant in his own right and seemed to be aware of everything going on around him. No doubt, he noticed similar traits in Melvin. Him being observant likely also included understanding how much the lab meant to Melvin.

But not all Melvin's secrets were shared. He kept his prized place secret from everyone until he met Pal. Most would end up simply wanting to reduce the lab to nothing by looting it and selling or trading everything inside.

Pal did not, which was why Melvin shared with him the knowledge of his lab.

Although Pal couldn't understand all of Melvin's work, he definitely appreciated how important the lab was. He didn't want to take any of it from Melvin or even expose what he did down here. He understood that much, or at least did his best to try.

It was beneficial to have Ash watching over the place during the brief times when he was above. On the surface of the flat.

The common emerger thought of the lab's contents as worthless, or worth selling, which was the opposite. Others simply could not appreciate everything that was possible within. If he were being honest, even he was still figuring things out, and it had been years since its discovery.

Melvin and Pal had wanted to work together when they first met. And that was even before Melvin informed him of the lab. Their cohesiveness was the result of them both having similar motivations: to better themselves, but also Home.

After Pal learned of some of Melvin's accomplishments, he respected him, and although he admitted he didn't understand the details, he believed in the experiments. And he was being truthful. Melvin could tell.

Melvin wouldn't have been able to do what Pal could either, even when he was younger; bringing people together no matter how much they hated one another before-hand. Hardly anyone could. It was one of the main reasons why Melvin wanted to associate with him.

Melvin believed, for a time, maybe he could learn to do the same. But alas, he could not. He simply didn't have the personality traits to inspire people as well. And being highly intelligent meant he was smart enough to know when or where he was weak at something.

He learned that working with someone who was good at what he was weak at, sometimes allowed him to overcome the weakness and instead be good at it.

So in a way, and in another of his experiments, Melvin brought emergers together, and Pal worked for him in his lab.

"I get worked up sometimes. I admit it. Easy to do in my old age. But one thing I appreciate about him is he doesn't judge me, us, even though some would consider our work cruel, maybe even evil. The judgment is by those who deserve death. *His* impartial view is appreciated. Trust between business partners is the foundation for success for all participants. And if you're successful enough, everyone can be considered as one."

Aside from Melvin's main experiments, he was paid currency by Pal for some side work he wanted done for himself, even though currency wasn't much use to Melvin considering he didn't voyage into towns much anymore. He didn't have much interest in going anymore either.

Currency wasn't useful to him personally, he didn't clamor over it or desire it as everyone did, but it was—ironically—necessary when he needed something from others. Currency did have perceived power.

Useful for bribery, brainwashing, and taking advantage of people. Especially when they were weak.

It was much easier to get someone to do something against their character, if they were paid enough.

Not everyone, but some could forget about the unspeakable demand asked of them. Stealing, killing, or even abducting people.

Excitement shot through him at the thought, and he squeezed the mic. "This is Melvin, over."

10. ROYAH

Onnin was carrying Emma. He didn't use the front pack baby carrier she offered. He preferred to hold her in the crook of a muscular forearm. He caught up with them and obviously wanted to listen.

To keep a better eye on things. Or maybe he just wanted to be nearer. To feel part of the group. If Royah thought Buddy was useful, then Onnin obviously didn't have a problem with him.

Royah had asked Onnin to carry Emma a few hours ago and he didn't seem to mind because he hadn't offered to give her back yet. Not that carrying a little baby would be difficult for such a man.

When he first held her, he would give her back after about a half hour or so but the more often Royah requested the relief, the longer he obliged her. She even caught him smiling down at her a few times, but it vanished once he'd been spotted.

It was a little after noon. An ancestor decided what time it was long ago. Royah often checked her timepiece repeatedly out of habit, to calculate when it would be dark.

She did it all the time when she lived in Westo out of boredom but now she was doing something substantial, and it was important to know what time it was for safety reasons. Night was far more dangerous than day.

It was still a few hours from night but she took the timepiece off and placed it in a pocket in her space suit, realizing its shine might be spotted. Then she rubbed her wrist.

She hoped her realization that it was glinting, might not have caused dangerous outliers to notice them already.

"I can always hold her too," Buddy said to Onnin.

Onnin gave him an irritated look.

"You'll get used to me eventually. Everybody does, so you might as well start now."

Onnin acted as though he hadn't even heard him.

Buddy turned his attention to Royah. "Hmm?"

"What?"

"You look like you have something you want to ask. And conversation helps pass the time."

Royah disguised her intent as best she could. "I suppose."

She had lots of questions for Buddy, but time would answer the most important of them, which was whether or not he could really be trusted.

Royah was nervous about how much she trusted Onnin already during such a short time period, and she thought she should force herself to be wary no matter how she felt.

But she really wanted to trust Onnin, and rely on Buddy the same way. It made her wonder about herself and if her instincts were reliable. It was a fear.

To think things in mere days? To feel so strongly seemed too soon. She wanted some reaffirmation, but being blunt could put people off. Or hurt feelings depending on who it was or what was being asked. Especially if the question came out like an accusation.

Royah just wanted to be sure. But surety might prove to be impossible. She supposed it was best to rely on her instincts, as she was doing now. Not that she had a choice.

"Come on. What do you want to know?"

"The town. The one you grew up in. Why did you leave?"

"No choice."

"There's always a choice."

"True, but *everyone* left. Outliers showed up, started harassing everyone and worse. There were robberies at first, fistfights, then murders. It was complete chaos. People got scared and started fleeing. Once they were gone, outliers took over completely."

He shook his head. His friendly demeanor was gone.

"I didn't mean to pry."

"That's all right. We don't know each other well yet."

"Unfortunately things like that happen too often."

"You're not kidding. Don't I know it. Anyway, I suppose I wanted to tell you guys."

Royah liked he included Onnin. "With all the bad going on there, when exactly did you leave?"

"As they started killing people left and right. Bargaining for those who couldn't go anywhere because they were too old or crippled or too stubborn to move elsewhere. They couldn't believe what was happening."

Buddy's eyes dug into the ground. They looked like they could do as much damage as the pistol holstered on his hip. His eyes rose up.

"They're just kids. It's what one of the old people said. Before he got shot. I felt bad for him. He hoped they would change. Turn good somehow."

"You're still a young man yourself. You must have been just a boy back then. You still are really."

Buddy blushed, and Onnin cracked off a muffled laugh.

Buddy obviously didn't like her calling him a boy, even though he was indeed young, probably in his twenties. No man would. She didn't mean anything by it but he didn't like it, so she wouldn't say it again.

Unless it accidentally slipped out. Sometimes she said things accidentally when she was nervous.

"I can handle myself." Buddy spotted Onnin's fading smirk and glared. "What about him? The baby carrier. Can he?"

"Can he what?"

"Handle himself."

Onnin was silent as he walked next to them, but his patience was obviously being tried. He was glaring, and it made Royah nervous.

You shouldn't push him.

But maybe doing so was how they would bond. There wasn't an alternative.

Let them be who they are.

"He can speak. Why don't you ask?"

"I thought you said don't ask him anything."

"We know you better now. You can try."

Buddy looked up at Onnin. "I've seen emergers before. But none like you."

Onnin said nothing.

"That's it?" Royah said. "That's your attempt at conversation? That's no way to go about it."

Buddy shrugged. "It's not my fault. I can't think of anything to say."

She wondered if this was going to work.

Here goes.

"What's the scariest story you ever heard about our companion?"

Onnin looked over at Royah. She gave him a wink, but she wasn't sure if he understood what she was doing. Attempting to do.

Buddy didn't hesitate. "He's twenty feet tall, which obviously isn't true. There are a lot more I guess. But scary ones? I'm not afraid of anybody with a baby."

"Brave little man." Onnin's voice was deep and gravelly. "You wouldn't be with us at all if it weren't for Royah. She doesn't think of you the way you want. And she never will. You're too young and too small."

"Size doesn't matter to a woman."

"It does out here. You're weak."

Buddy's face scrunched. "Just because I'm short, doesn't mean...You think I'm weak, huh? We'll see."

Buddy walked faster, charging ahead. It was Royah's turn to look at Onnin but he was expressionless. Royah was around men long enough to know how they interacted. They could be quite rough on each other, even when they were joking. Neighbors in Westo came to mind.

But often, they ended up as friends. Or at least friendly enough to get along. As long as they didn't kill each other.

Onnin was being defensive and probably didn't mean to be so harsh, but he was responding to Buddy the same way he was talking, same tone. From what she knew about Onnin already, he wasn't the type to back down from a fight.

"This is my fault. I was trying to..." Royah paused. "It was an attempt to get our fears about one another out in the open. I think it's pretty obvious the stories about Onnin aren't true."

"You don't know that," Onnin said.

Can't you tell what I'm trying to do?

"Both of you have been through this kind of thing before and I want you to get along. I don't want what I've seen other men do to each other, to happen."

"Which is what?" Buddy called back to her.

"Well, some people think if they can get away with something, they might as well try to get away with even more. It's natural, especially for the young. They constantly test boundaries."

"I'm not young!" Buddy hollered. "Unbelievable."

"I just wanted to get things out into the open." She noticed Onnin wasn't so tense at her side. "So they don't come up unexpectedly later."

11. ROYAH

For a while, it seemed like Buddy might go his own way. But eventually he sided up next to them once again. And he no longer seemed so frustrated.

The next few hours, not much was said between the three of them. Especially between Onnin and Buddy. They scarcely even looked in each other's direction. It almost seemed they might get into a fight for no reason other than they were both men.

Men of different ages. That probably had something to do with it. Royah wasn't a man, so she didn't fully understand the behavior. She sighed.

Once again, Royah was backpacking Emma on her front, which she didn't mind doing. She knew she could ask Onnin to carry her whenever she wanted and maybe even Buddy, but she felt fine holding her. Plus, she was enjoying it more and more.

The sun was hot overhead in the late afternoon. Wavy heat crawled toward mountains in the distance, interspersed with sporadic bodies of water. The lakes twinkled. It was said that runoff from the mountains pooled from underground.

She wasn't sure how anyone could know. The vastness of the flat grew exponentially when she stared long enough. Large mountain peaks loomed in the distance, but looked to be so far away, they could be mistaken for other planets.

The thought of the attempt on foot made her thirsty, so, careful of Emma, she took a swig from her canteen.

Lakes formed either from underground as was said, or, another belief, by others, were remnants of rivers. Whenever anyone ran low on water, they filled their canteens up from any of the lakes.

Regardless of their creation, lakes were a reliable drinking source, since there were so many between the quadrants. It was unknown, but likely, that there were lakes stretching across Planet Home. Where outliers considered home.

When desperate to quench thirst, all anyone needed to do was cup hands together, dunk, and drink. Except it was safest to keep a canteen full.

There were rumors—over the net—some outliers, the worst kind, waited underwater breathing through old tech waiting to grab somebody, anyone, and pull them beneath the surface to drown them. Then they would eat them later.

The thought made Royah shiver even under the hot sun. The silence of Home was deafening except for when wind kicked up, blowing so strongly they often needed to cover their eyes.

The occasional dust storm wasn't a hindrance per say, because they were so infrequent, but sometimes they needed to stop and wait until it was over.

It was then that Royah wished she had kept the helmet completing her space suit as opposed to burying it. Except it had been a way to show trust in Onnin. If he didn't wear a helmet, why would she?

Buddy resumed putting distance between Onnin and even herself. He was leading the trek. For a while, it seemed he reconsidered and might actually leave them behind. No doubt multiple thoughts played in his mind.

Onnin acted as if it would be fine with him if Buddy left, but it couldn't be what even he wanted. The more members in the group, the more who could fight if there was a skirmish.

If Buddy actually did attempt to leave, Royah would call out to him and ask him to stay. She wasn't quite sure how she would word it but she would do something if it were necessary. And she wouldn't do it in a way making him think she was interested in him romantically.

It wouldn't be fair to put false ideas in his head because she wasn't interested in him that way, which was how men often wanted women to behave toward them. Often men weren't interested only in being friends with a woman.

She genuinely liked Buddy. Enough to want him around for the quest. But only as a friend. Onnin on the other hand was a different story.

There was definitely something between her and him. She wasn't even remotely close to being able to identify what it was exactly. Her feelings had feelings of their own. She didn't know how to approach it with him. If at all.

She wasn't sure what it was or what it meant, but it felt new. Interesting, because although they hadn't talked much, Onnin seemed familiar. Warm and pleasant and comfortable but in ways she couldn't quite put her finger on, because she'd never felt that way before.

Her feelings weren't the result of the time spent together, so they must be more than an ordinary crush. She knew him for about as long as she'd known Buddy. Onnin had remained pretty much silent since Buddy joined them, so it must be a bond deeper than words.

Even so, and understanding what was happening—seeming impossible—Royah was drawn to Onnin in ways that occurred few times during her life. She'd never even spent time with the objects of her affections, just some playful words back and forth.

The feelings were probably mutual, but she was just a kid then. A young woman. Now she was grown.

What would she do if she knew them today? She wondered, excitedly, in a way making her nervous at the same time because she realized it was happening again. It was happening right now.

She exhaled. Nothing could be done about it today. Not during the quest. Maybe not ever. But it didn't mean that she couldn't play with the outcome in her mind.

If she were to explain herself, and Onnin felt the same way as she did, would he know what to do about it? Would she? He was older than her but still seemed inexperienced. She could sense it.

Time would tell what might happen. Between them. As of right now, they were in no position to pursue anything resembling a romantic relationship. There was far too much going on.

Too much danger. She refocused.

Must concentrate on the path in front of her. There was still much of the map between here and AD. And too many things could go wrong.

Then again, maybe she was making excuses because she was afraid of getting close to someone. She had the right to feel that way. No man ever really loved her because she never allowed herself to love. Too scary. Realistically, so far it had only been lust.

As they walked on, the gap between them eventually shrank and then disappeared altogether. Nothing like a little time to get over uncomfortable feelings, especially between people who didn't know one another very well.

Buddy obviously got over whatever he had been feeling. A calmness emanated from him. Then he suddenly bent down close to the ground and looked as if he were resting, except his hands were busy doing something.

Royah couldn't tell, so she slid Emma slightly as she was obscuring her view, and then she saw Onnin put his hand on the butt of his revolver.

As they approached where Buddy was waiting for them, he suddenly thrust something toward Royah, and Onnin quick-drew his revolver, leveling it at Buddy's head.

"Whoa!" Buddy was holding protein plant leaves. "For the lady."

Onnin lowered his gun and cursed silently, then blinked with confusion. Royah slowly got over almost having a heart attack.

"Everybody's so jumpy all of the sudden. Glad you have control over your trigger finger, big guy." Buddy lowered his hands. "Don't shoot."

Buddy slowly approached Royah and presented the bouquet. It was obviously a romantic gesture, surely not lost on Onnin, but especially not to Royah. The custom of giving a gift preceding a courtship was common on Earth except it was done with flowers there.

There were no flowers here, but the custom endured even on other planets. Somehow. Including Home.

She forced herself to react, feeling uncomfortable but also flattered at the same time. "Oh, thank you. It's pretty."

Buddy glanced defiantly at Onnin. Even though Royah wasn't interested in Buddy, and he made it clear how he felt about her without the possibility of reciprocation, it still gave her a rush to be presented with such a gift.

She couldn't help feeling flattered. She'd never been given a courtship gift before. Hardly been complimented either. She mostly witnessed the ugly side of men and any comments about her were typically aggressive ones about her body.

Nothing to do with getting to know who she was as a person. Glancing sideways at Onnin, she was suddenly embarrassed about the smile she couldn't prevent from spreading across her face.

Mostly because—although she couldn't be sure—Onnin seemed to be jealous. Although she didn't want him to feel that way, it somewhat reaffirmed how she was feeling about him.

All of this was quite confusing while making sense at the same time. Onnin obviously didn't think much of Buddy at first. He was shorter than him with a young man's energy he was clearly annoyed by.

She needed Onnin's help and didn't want him to feel frustrated and leave, but Buddy was persistent. Even though she didn't have feelings for him, she still enjoyed the attention.

What was a girl to do?

It was sort of silly but she brought the plants close and sniffed them, as she imagined the women of Earth did when receiving such a gift of affection. As she did, Buddy smiled.

12. ONNIN

Buddy's smile vanished, and as he dodged right, Onnin's jealousy faltered. Especially when Buddy yanked his pistol out of its holster and aimed.

Onnin instinctively ducked, yanking out his revolver, aiming it at Buddy, and Royah clutched Emma to her chest and dropped the bouquet, the leaves spearing toward the ground in different directions.

Trust Buddy and now this?

The yellow sizzle from Buddy's gun fired across the flat and echoed.

Onnin nearly pulled the trigger, but Buddy's gunblast had missed him by a mile. The shot hadn't even come close. What was peculiar was Buddy's claim to have skill with a gun. Skill wasn't required to shoot Onnin from such a short distance, especially with him being so big.

Then Buddy fired again and missed Onnin for a second time. Instead of reacting with his revolver, Onnin twisted to look.

There was a dead man in the distance. Buddy hadn't been trying to harm him, he was protecting him.

"Told you," Buddy lowered his gun and holstered it. "Great shot."

Onnin marched over and stared down at the dead man. More of an examination, trying to see if he recognized him. Deduce his threat level. Also, get over his embarrassment of being distracted by jealousy.

"You know him?" Buddy called out.

Onnin shook his head.

"What's wrong?"

"He has a look of desperation."

"So?"

Onnin raised his voice so they could hear him as well as if he were standing right next to them. "He didn't want to die."

Buddy laughed. "Most don't!"

"Fighting off death was a struggle. He didn't mean to be spotted. He was a scout."

"Who was armed!"

Although Onnin easily made his deep voice heard, Royah needed to shout as Buddy did. "What does that mean?"

"There's more of them. And they're headed this way." Onnin pointed. "Look."

Buddy squinted. "I don't see anything."

"Then you'll have to wait. Will both of you come to me please?"

They did.

Buddy didn't take his eyes away from the distance. "You can see them?"

Onnin ignored Buddy and looked to Royah and pointed, but she shook her head. She couldn't see anyone either.

He waited, and eventually small shapes grew larger on the flat as the minutes went by. Soon they were visible to all of them and, unfortunately, it was obvious they were walking toward them.

"See?"

"Yeah," Royah said. "Buddy?"

"Now I do." Buddy turned to Onnin. "Man, you have good eyesight."

"What's your kill range?"

"Definitely closer. Sorry, big guy. What about you?"

"If I can see them I can hit them. But for you, we'll wait."

"Hey, I can—"

"It wasn't a slight. We have women to protect."

Buddy relaxed. "You're right."

Onnin was somewhat taken aback by his own sudden transformation. Minutes ago, he was prepared to kill Buddy, but it had been a misunderstanding, and now they were once again allies.

Buddy behaved like a different person entirely. All it took was some danger. The young, annoying, insecure man hoping for Royah's affection was gone in an instant, and now he was a gunfighter.

Onnin hardly recognized him. Determined eyes, intense face, and pursed lips. He'd seen the look before.

Onnin holstered his revolver and swung his rifle from around his wide back and aimed it. "Just looking."

Royah leaned toward him. "How many more are there?"

Onnin hesitated to make sure. "Three."

Royah gave the emaciated dead man a better look too. Probably he'd been starving. Him and the people closing in on them were probably all just as desperate.

He'd been able to sneak up on them because Onnin and Buddy were arguing. He was so thin that he probably didn't weigh more than a child even though he was an adult.

"Why's he so skinny?" she said. "There are plants everywhere."

Buddy didn't take his eyes off the approaching group. "Maybe he's sick."

"Halt," Onnin shouted, "or we'll shoot!"

Normally he prevented his voice from booming—causing Buddy and Royah to startle, and Emma to cry—but it was necessary.

Royah did her best to soothe her. "Next time you yell, a little warning first?"

Onnin nodded curtly.

Buddy pulled his pistol from its holster once again. "They aren't stopping."

Onnin was completely still as he scanned the distance. Then he fired a yellow warning shot over their heads. The gunblast echoed across the flat. It didn't deter their approach. In fact, they proceeded as if they were deaf.

"Outliers," Buddy said. "The worst."

"No," Onnin said. "There are worse."

"Who could possibly be worse?"

Onnin decided to say nothing more about it.

"You've got the rifle. Kill them."

Onnin's respect for Buddy evaporated under the circumstances. "Don't tell me what to do, boy."

The outliers pace didn't slow up. If they were smart, they would have at least spread out. They seemed willing to take risks.

For what though? Water, a meal, supplies? They must have been willing to die for whatever it was they desired, otherwise they would have heeded his warning.

"Shoot them already!"

Royah jostled Emma in the front pack as she continued to try to get her to calm down. "Maybe we can give them some food and they'll move on."

"Their guns are out, Royah. Even I can see that. Can't you?"

"Yes, but—"

Buddy raised his pistol. "We killed one of their people. You're holding a baby. We have supplies of value and we're on an important quest. We have to fight now."

Onnin tore away his view from the incoming threat, briefly. "Royah, get behind me."

Royah hurried over to Onnin, now completely obscured by his massive bulk. Onnin glanced behind him, making sure he knew where his friends were, then he turned his head and was as still as his aim.

He lever-actioned his rifle, and every time he squeezed the trigger, the yellow bursts of energy shooting across the flat. Firing three times, every shot dropped an outlier in the distance.

The gunblasts echoed across Home, followed by a light wind.

Royah took her hands off Emma's ears. Emma sniffled in tiny little fits, ready to fall asleep again. Two of the dead were on their backs in the distance. They were the first ones Onnin shot.

The last was face down because he tried to run away. All of their wounds had been dead center. Buddy claimed to be a great shot, but Onnin definitely was. The dead were proof.

13. ROYAH

“What now?” she said.

Buddy sided up next to Royah, protecting her too. “What do you mean? We’re still going, right?”

“Of course. I meant...Onnin?”

Onnin continued to look down the sights of his rifle. “We must wait.”

Buddy looked over and up at him. “Will you be able to tell if there are more?”

“What do you think?”

Buddy rolled his eyes. “Just tell us when it’s clear.”

“Home is never clear.”

“You know what I meant. They didn’t even return fire.”

Royah covered Emma’s ears again. “Should we bury the bodies?”

Onnin shook his head. “No. In case more come.”

Royah looked out, staring, then even left and right as far as she could see. “See anyone?”

Onnin remained silent as he scanned the distance.

“Is she all right?” Buddy said to Royah. “She’s so quiet all of a sudden.”

Royah petted Emma’s tiny head. “I think so.”

“How about you?”

“Me? I’m good. But I dropped your gift. I’m sorry.”

“It’s okay.” Buddy’s smile vanished when he glanced at his combat partner. “How about it?”

Onnin lowered his rifle. Without looking over and down at him, he shook his head.

“Press on right?”

"Right," Onnin grumbled.

Royah averted Emma's view of the nearest dead man, and Buddy immediately headed in their original direction. Emma was a baby but no one, no matter what age, should see such a disturbing sight if it was avoidable.

Once they put the shooting behind them, and they'd been traveling for a few hours, and none of them were talking, the windy silence between them must have finally bothered Buddy because he kept looking in Royah's direction.

"Something's on your mind."

"A mystery."

"What mystery?"

"*The* mystery. I've been trying to solve it by asking fellow emergers their opinion for a long time."

Buddy hadn't been the only one tired of the quiet. Royah was glad. She was in the mood to talk too. Anything to get her mind off the killings.

"Opinion about what?"

"The greatest mystery of Home."

"You listening, Onnin?"

"Yes."

"Go ahead. Enlighten us."

Buddy grinned. "Are you making fun of me?"

"You're being so serious." Royah adjusted Emma. "It doesn't matter what we talk about. Anything but what happened back there."

Buddy pointed around them. "Do either of you know what happened to Home?"

"You mean the destruction? The war happened. Everyone knows that. There were great battles between two sides and they annihilated each other. Some of those people survived and we're their offspring."

"Those two sides. Do you know *who* they were?"

"Not exactly. Two armies. Or one army and they fought the colonists. I've even heard the colonists weren't involved. But it didn't save them. Then again, I've heard all kinds of stories."

"What about you, Onnin?"

Onnin shook his head. He continued to stare straight ahead as if their destination was already in view. His reaction was a little too quick for her to think he wasn't thinking about something serious.

She also got the feeling that he knew something about what they were talking about. But he didn't want to say what it was.

How well traveled is he?

"There was a war, but not the way you described."

Her attention returned to the conversation. She chuckled. How could he know? "What do you mean?"

"I wasn't going to say anything. I don't even know how much of it matters. But we've been through battle together. That means a lot to me. I trust you both."

Royah didn't have to look at Onnin to know he was rolling his eyes now. "We're intrigued."

"I'll tell you what I know."

Onnin cleared his throat. "During our lifetime?"

Buddy snickered. "It wasn't a *who.* It was a *what.*"

"What?"

"I'm not the only one who thinks so either. Others I've talked to, told me the same thing. I've also heard about it over the net many, many times."

Royah squinted. "How about you tell *us.*"

Buddy opened his mouth. About to explain. He grinned instead. "Actually we're close enough. It'll be easier if I show you. You both okay with deviating from our path a little ways?"

Royah shot Onnin a look. He nodded. So she said, "Sure."

Buddy quickened his pace. "Follow me."

14. MELVIN

The currency was useful at times because of necessary expenditures. Unfortunately, the experiments required assistance. He didn't have everything required at all times for he could not foresee the future.

When he didn't have all the elements in the lab that were necessary, he contacted whoever was manning the radio on Pal's people's end, gave them a description of what he required for his latest research, and then had it delivered. Away from the lab of course.

Once again an opportunity to give a directionless outlier, a purpose. The business relationship between him and Pal accomplished many things.

Melvin was able to continue his work, his experiments providing the army functionality by currency. It inspired a work ethic allowing those he was forced to depend on to be more reliable. And it was a potential bond Melvin might exploit in the future if necessary.

Even though it couldn't be farther from the truth, many attributed Melvin as part of Pal's army. Though he technically worked for Pal considering Pal paid him, Melvin did not consider himself to be one of his outliers.

Almost all of the work he accomplished was for himself aside from some side tests if requested, and reported a *few* new discoveries.

Radios were open frequency, so it was important he didn't divulge important aspects over the net. If he made the mistake, some might realize he was responsible for the deaths of their relatives. He needed almost everything he did to remain a secret.

Pal was smart enough to understand that, so when it was necessary, and Melvin didn't feel comfortable talking over the net, they met face to face.

For all other communication, like what he required for certain experimentation, he divulged over the radio because he was asked to. It was a tactic.

Whoever was listening couldn't understand the complications of his processes because they lacked the intellect, and also he was selective about what he divulged. Difficult to understand the eighth step with two and three and five missing.

It was believed by Pal that the more emergers perceived as working for him, the more powerful he would seem to those listening, and thus would inspire even more to join him. It was a way of not only retaining his power, but also building upon it simultaneously.

Melvin obliged him—it was an interesting strategy and it was working—but he still held a few secrets for himself. It would always be that way.

The correspondence by radio between them took place at least once a week at Pal's recommendation. Occasionally twice. Pal never insisted on it, not exactly. As he put it, it was a productive idea.

Though it gave Melvin little choice, he knew it was one of the many ways Pal enforced his power, which kept Melvin's own work going with momentum in his old age, and in turn maintained their partnership.

"Mutual. Even though I'm being manipulated, I allow it. He thinks the corresponding updates are his idea. I don't tell him everything of course. Besides, he wouldn't be able to figure out half of what we do down here. Even if he knew what to look for. And at my age, our age, we deserve privacy no matter how much currency we're paid."

Melvin waited for a response. Of course there wasn't one.

Ash worked in silence as much as Melvin did and Melvin respected Ash's privacy in return. Sometimes he got the feeling that Ash didn't believe what he told him. He was smart to do so.

Melvin sometimes lied.

The updates over the net were Pal's suggestion but Melvin's lab partner didn't need to know every aspect. Melvin's manipulation even grew into his partnership with the one person he trusted. Other than himself.

"Why do I even talk to you? You think you understand me because we've worked together for so long? I know more than I let on."

More often than not, talking to Ash was a waste of time. He almost never contributed anything. Except silent judgment.

Still, Melvin often learned from it and appreciated his loyalty. Having a partner, especially down in the lab, someone to talk to, comforted him. It allowed him to bounce ideas off someone.

What was I thinking about?

"Our work!"

With everything he tackled each day, the research piquing his interest lately was the Alien. It fascinated him more than almost everything in the lab aside from the war document and for more reasons than he could list. He was intrigued by it even though it hardly moved.

The research itself wasn't complicated and may have been why it was one of his favorites.

Thinking about the Alien relaxed him, observing it a hobby, and was yet an additional reason Melvin wished he would live for another hundred years, to see what it might do, if anything. He yearned for answers lying in wait.

Although material possessions meant as much to him as science did to the average outlier, he contrarily took great care of his radio. Maintaining it was a distraction and a minor annoyance but a necessary task.

Although he despised the ridiculous gossip the radio was often used for, so much power was possible over the net. And it all began by doing something as simple as pressing a mic.

Though his plans were much more important than mere radio maintenance, even he had to devote time to such a chore. Necessary, but as arduous as hygiene. He had even discovered the radio within the pristine confines of the science lab.

It hadn't been destroyed by the war, which was a rarity. Almost everything else—machines, weapons, and structures—were reduced to nothingness.

The lab and everything in it changed his life. For however long the rest of it might be. And also for the better. It revealed his true identity, what he discovered there about himself. It had been waiting for him to find it all those years.

Spending most of his time in his lab and possessing technology allowing him to contact above ground, made his life ideal. His main use of the net was communication, but even he suffered from curiosity. He would often listen in on other frequencies before he forced himself to sleep.

Except he never wanted to close his eyes, there was always so much to do, but unfortunately he was human.

The benefit of being older—one of the benefits he could think of, aside from the innocent initially believing him—was that he found he needed less sleep than when he was a young man. He could get away with four- or five hours each night. Sometimes just three.

There were many frequencies on the net, a few thousand, as scattered as dwellings, so it was difficult to listen to them all. Over time, each one, yes, but he could only devote a few minutes to them because he also needed to conduct his experiments.

Such a short time was hardly enough to get the gist over the open net about what was going on everywhere else. The main frequency he listened to, mostly, ironically, was the same one he'd been trying to get a response on over the last few days.

Pal's plots were suspicious to say the least. Melvin thought a man like him would be much more cautious, encourage communication on varying frequencies for each correspondence, so his secrets would remain so. Except, he obviously wanted something else to occur.

He wanted open broadcasts, as many ears listening to what he and everyone else he was involved with were saying as possible. The reason, Melvin knew, was that he was constantly recruiting for his army.

"Similar to myself, he must have realized secrecy in the form of communication on Home using radios envisioned for wartime, was impossible. So, he embraced its flaws and his plan has worked wonders for him. His broadcasts are so optimistic, I find them rather comical. Maybe it's my age. But obviously not to the desperate ears of outliers, who are lost and searching for meaning and a sense of purpose."

Melvin stood and raised his thin arms up in the air into an uncomfortable, necessary stretch before sitting back down.

"Outliers listen because he tells them what they want to hear. They embrace what he has to say, thinking he has the answers. He's the one who can fix everything, what they ruined for themselves, and they even encourage others to do the same. Then they show up in droves. It's quite brilliant."

He coughed and cleared his throat.

"He's conducting his own experiment, but doesn't even realize it. He also doesn't know I've secretly involved us in the experiment. To understand where the tipping point is for emergers, to embrace something new, then abandon all they know. Fascinating. No, I'm not talking too much!"

Ash acted worried about Melvin's overexertion. It was obvious the competition between them won out. They were partners, but also both masked loathing of the other. Melvin was sure Ash was busily studying him by mentally judging his health.

Of course Melvin would never reveal that he appreciated the competition and intended to best Ash at the end, which was to live longer, something he'd already done. The way to continue was not to reveal his knowledge.

Not in any way. To act normally.

"His popularity is going to his head no doubt and it carries over to how he treats others. Everyone thinks as highly of him as his gullible army. He pretends to be interested in everything I'm working on and acts excited about what I'm talking about, but his interest is feigned."

Melvin waited to see if Ash would react. He did not.

15. MELVIN

"He cares about two aspects of my, our, work: war research and his progress on cultivating something to eat other than protein plants. Because they're dying out. The man is building an army, working day and night—he hardly sleeps—because what he desires is to sit down and enjoy a dinner of old."

Melvin laughed out loud. He couldn't stop himself. It was quite funny.

A man like Pal, probably the most powerful man on the planet, and his main goal was to have a meal as people enjoyed on Earth. His underlings discovered many pictures, advertisements, and information on what those things were.

The colonists and the Lokis—technically—died off and left it all behind, but their existence was hundreds of years ahead of Earthlings. They may have even experienced the luxuries for themselves.

It was close enough for Pal to believe he could one day do the same. He probably wanted to indulge in one of those meals above those he ruled. It was Melvin's private joke.

The thought of cooked meat made Melvin's mouth water, which was fascinating because he'd never eaten animal flesh. But he'd seen pictures. He too, like many, was beyond sick of eating protein plants every single day for almost every single meal for their entire life.

Though many years away from Earth compared to today, emergers still craved what was popular, and necessary, sustenance. It was in all human genes somehow.

"The experiences of our ancestors somehow get passed down to descendants in surprising ways."

There was one other option, other than miraculously reinventing animals to eat on this planet, something he'd even considered for a short time when he was younger during his experiments near Orthal.

Especially seeing how others reacted to the bodies, the meat of those they killed, but he'd decided against cannibalism.

There were no animals on Home as there were on Earth. Just plants and people and the Alien. Protein plants, though gag inducing if too much was consumed—sometimes Melvin threw up what he ate—were a flawed but magnificent invention.

Invented by the colonists before the war, protein plants weren't only a food source, but they also produced oxygen, and contributed toward and sustained the initial terraforming efforts by the first people to set foot here.

What they established continued to this day. The question was, for how much longer?

After he squeezed his eyes shut, trying to eliminate the mental strain forming somewhere at the front of his skull, he stared at the radio. It'd been hours since his last attempt.

He squeezed the mic. "This is Melvin, over."

Flipping his thumb off, hearing open net, he sighed. Seemed there would be a lot more time for him to think on the things he liked to think about. Before there would be a response.

It would likely be this way for the rest of his life; waiting for outliers to somehow become civilized enough to answer him in the timely manner he deserved. It definitely would be a fine way to illustrate deserved respect.

Melvin glanced to see if Ash could see what he was about to do. Satisfied he could not and facing away, he quietly opened a drawer.

From his desk, he removed the document he'd discovered. It was a prized possession and war research. No one knew about it but himself, Ash—Ash was never allowed to read it, but Melvin read some of it to him—and possibly Pal.

Melvin caught Pal holding the envelope once. It was before Melvin performed the surgery. He knew Pal liked to snoop and was quite sneaky, but he was pretty sure Pal hadn't read it. At least not in its entirety.

If he had, then he was a better liar than Melvin knew him to be. Either way, they were working together, so Melvin could live with it. Besides, Melvin had discovered plenty of noteworthy documents.

In another one, he read about an attack on Earth by a man who experimented with hormones. He'd injected himself with a concoction, an engineered dose of what already resided within humans, and walked into the middle of a city.

A riot was the result. Everyone turned against one another, devolving into a primal mob. The scientist, who was termed a terrorist, had learned of ways to manipulate hormones in human beings and control their behavior.

According to the detailed articles—Melvin wished there was far more depth—the scientist could separate and identify hormones, thus he was able to wield humans like weapons by using what already dwelled inside them.

No need for conventional obliteration devices like the ones used during the war on this planet, but simply the nature of human beings being manipulated.

Most would likely think of the scientist as he was named, a terrorist, but Melvin thought of him as someone who wanted to advance the human species and also understand it. Melvin would have liked to have been able to converse with him about his research.

Unfortunately, that would have been impossible. He'd been torn limb from limb by the mob he'd created. Melvin would have even settled for speaking with the author. It seemed he knew nearly as much about what transpired as the scientist who was torn to pieces.

The author culminated all the scientist's research. Then he finished the documentation with accounts from witnesses and news reports. Actually broadcasted with a global communication tech similar to the net here on Home, but there it could be watched.

What a fascinating experiment.

The war document was what interested Melvin currently, and it had been written by a journalist. The journalist never referred to himself by name. He'd ended up planning on keeping his knowledge to himself, for the future, to be a classified reference but it didn't happen.

Not the way he envisioned. Whoever he was, died, and Melvin rediscovered his efforts. Now his knowledge had become his. To possess something so substantial and important made him feel powerful.

He hadn't wanted to damage the document itself, so he used a pencil to write ANONYMOUS on the outside of the yellow envelope in which the document was discovered.

It was Melvin's contribution and further proof that his work was meaningful. Melvin's understanding likely went against what the Lokis' leaders intended.

The supplicating papers explained a colonel from a branch of military was directly responsible for annihilating the civilization here—the drones finished the job.

Before a few lucky emergers rose out of the destruction, Home had been chosen as a testing ground for the latest weaponry, training, tactics, and top secret biological technology.

Flourishing is what the colonists likely envisioned upon first discovering the planet, before it was Home, to the soldiers, but they were deceived. If no one set foot here, Home would have remained a lifeless rock.

He placed the document on his desk to read later. Poring over the account was something he did hundreds of times already but always looked forward to the next time. Especially, as he waited for a response over the net.

Considering how long it typically took someone to get back to him, he'd likely be able to read it a few hundred more times.

Saving what he looked forward to, he allowed himself to get lost in other thoughts, aloud, for Ash.

"The colonists would have introduced wildlife to Home eventually. It is likely they were in possession of genes from the animals from Earth and the capability to create them. That's obvious with what I discovered myself. But they were mostly killed off by the drones, so nearly everything they'd brought with them was destroyed also. Make sense?"

He waited.

"Oh, you're a big help."

Trying to locate even hints of where such data might be, was one of his main objectives whenever he went above to the surface each morning. As he kept his radio pristine, he also maintained his scoutbike in the same fashion.

He never found a trace of the evidence he and others suspected existed, but he would scour Home no matter how long it took. It would be his life's work to bring some more of Earth to Home, aside from its destructive weapons.

With actual genetic tissue, there would be all kinds of interesting possibilities. Ones some might judge as immoral. Yet it would bring him so much more power. Power he deserved.

More than Pal did.

He squeezed the mic. "This is Melvin, over."

16. ROYAH

Conversation set the pace. Anything, even something they were pontificating about, seemed to take their minds off how tired they were from traveling on foot. And also, how much farther they must go on.

Only Onnin seemed unfazed. It seemed he could keep trudging forward for years. Doing what he'd likely done his entire life. It meant there was time to get to know him better, but she also wanted to obtain a scoutbike to alleviate the soreness from foot travel.

It got to the point where all three were taking turns carrying Emma. The help was necessary—for Royah—since Emma already gained weight from consistent feedings. With so much protein juice made, Royah was able to feed Emma whenever she was hungry. Emma was hungry often.

Better for everyone because the men didn't like it when she cried. They didn't say it, especially Onnin, but it probably made them feel sorry for her.

Also helpless to do anything about it, tapping into deep rooted instinct to protect, passed down by ancestors from Planet Earth. It was touching.

When Buddy carried Emma, he would say soothing things to her—even Onnin would whisper in a deep voice—and when the other one got tired, or more accurately, when Buddy got tired, Onnin would be ready to carry Emma again.

Onnin pretended to be ready to hand her over. When a substantial amount of time had passed. Pretended, as if he could no longer handle her weight. Royah suspected he was just trying to be normal. To fit in with them.

Except doing so, he was being abnormal. Onnin could have carried Emma for the entirety of the quest.

They would pass Emma back and forth until Royah wanted her again, which was entirely up to her. Or when it was time to change her or feed her. But even the men were now taking turns feeding her with the bottles filled with protein juice.

Royah never felt better in her life. Maybe it was because they were constantly on the move, or having the company of two interesting men, or acting as a mother. It was probably all of it. The quest was dangerous, but for some reason, she was enjoying every minute of it.

"So," Buddy said to Royah, "when are you going to tell me where you're *really* going?"

"Slingtown."

"And after? I've done enough to know. Seeing as we were in battle and all."

"Not much of a battle," Onnin said. "They didn't shoot back."

"Dangerous enough to almost get you killed had I not pulled my pistol."

Onnin looked over at him. "True. Thank you."

Buddy's eyes went wide and a smile followed. He put a hand to his ear.

"Don't push it."

Buddy laughed and dropped his hand. It smacked against his dusty pants. "Just reminding you, big guy. No offense. I have to know something though. With you being so big."

"With me being so big what?"

"I would think you'd be easy to shoot from a distance."

Royah scoffed. "Buddy!"

"Well, I was wondering what he thought about it."

Onnin seemed amused. "Most of the time, I see people before they see me. If they take a shot, first shots usually miss. Then it's my turn. I don't miss."

"Unless it's on purpose," Royah chimed in.

Onnin snorted.

Buddy's face scrunched. "What?"

"Nothing. Private joke."

"Ah. So, how about it?"

"How about what?"

"*Royah*."

"Why do you need to know everything?"

"I want to know what I'm risking my life for. We're obviously headed for a place marked on your map, what you hid from me when you held it up earlier. Covering it with your hand." He must have read her expression. "It's okay. I wouldn't trust me at first either."

"A-D."

"A-D, huh? What's it stand for?"

Royah shrugged.

"Is it the end of where you're going or is there more? You can tell me."

"I honestly don't know."

Buddy laughed. "That makes sense."

Royah looked over at Onnin. "I'm going to show him."

Onnin stared back at her and then nodded. Royah raised the necklace into view.

"I noticed it before. What is it?"

"It plugs into a machine."

"What kind of machine?"

Royah shrugged.

"What's it do?"

"The man who found it thinks it has information at its center."

"Like a book?"

"I suppose."

"Who found it?"

Onnin groaned. "Must you ask so many questions?"

"So you, we three, are on a mission, with a baby, risking our lives to get somewhere on a map and no one knows exactly where or why?"

Onnin's annoyance didn't falter. "Answer yourself this time."

Of course Buddy didn't understand. How could he? She hardly

understood herself. But she couldn't explain any more about it even if she wanted to.

Buddy should know what he was risking his life for, but, unfortunately, she had no new information to give. She was going with her gut and she'd convinced these men to go along with her. Hopefully that was enough. And they would continue to do so.

They all had purpose and she got the feeling a sense of purpose was what everyone needed. In one way or another.

She hoped they would find something more. A secret to solve many mysteries. It was fascinating that information might dwell within something the size of a thumb. And dangling from her neck.

"I'll tell you what I think," Buddy said. "Those responsible for the destruction have remained hidden, whoever and whatever they are and their motives are mysterious and secret. There are all kinds of rumors about what *they* are exactly. A lot of people think they're aliens."

"Really?"

"Really. Hmm. Well one thing we can agree on is that the first occupiers of Home were the colonists, right?"

"Sure."

"Right?" Buddy said to Onnin.

"I wasn't there."

"I'm not asking if you were—"

"You mentioned aliens. If so, how could colonists be the first to set foot on the planet? Especially considering where you're taking us."

"You're not just a big guy, but a smart guy too. But I didn't say the first to set foot here, I said occupiers."

Royah was genuinely curious. "Where's he taking us?"

Onnin stared at Buddy, and Buddy stared back using telepathy to tell Onnin what he was thinking.

"He'll show us."

"Thanks. Anyway, as I was saying, those who rose from the ashes of the war, from the ashes of those ruins, are referred to as emergers. We can all agree?"

Onnin nodded too.

"I like this. You're both hearing me out. You two aren't the only ones who know things. Even Emma's probably hanging on my every word."

Onnin was holding Emma at the moment. He held her up and moved her back and forth, as if she were shaking her head. Royah laughed and so did Buddy. Onnin even grinned. A little.

Buddy's laughter subsided. "We might as well pass the time by trying to figure it out. If we can."

Onnin held Emma close to his massive chest. "It won't change anything."

"I disagree. And how could knowing more not help with the quest?" Buddy opened his eyes dramatically. "*Whatever* it is."

Royah held her arms out for Emma, and Onnin passed her over. Emma snuggled into the front pack.

Onnin seemed comfortable with the conversation. Being open to listening to Buddy was huge for all of them. Mutual respect between the men was something she wanted for them since they'd met.

She wasn't sure if they'd realized it, but they'd gone from confrontational to making fun of each other. From what she knew about men, making fun of each other meant they were going to be best friends.

"Have either of you been to Westo?" she asked them.

"Maybe when I was young," Buddy said. "My parents could have brought me there but I don't remember, so probably not."

She looked up at Onnin.

"Near it."

"I think you would have noticed him," Buddy said.

Royah grew serious. "Westo's a solid place to get information because of the proclivity of gathering anything having to do with pre-war. Guns are everywhere but especially near my home town. A child could practically start digging and pull one out of the dirt."

She tried to remember.

"There was definitely a war. Irrefutable, based on the ruins and what's left of the planet. Maybe involving the colonists. Soldiers. Armies. Something destroyed both sides."

Buddy nodded. "Whatever it was, it hated people."

"The mystery of what they were and what they did and why, is still unknown. Some think they were terrorists."

"Terrorists. Like an additional group? Other than the colonists and soldiers?"

"Apparently."

"Maybe. But besides emergers, who else is there?" Buddy spread his arms out and it turned into a stretch. Then he yawned.

"Good idea," Royah said.

They stopped to rest.

Until Onnin cleared his throat, clearly hinting they should get moving again.

"Come on, big guy. It isn't night yet."

"A few more minutes?" Royah said. "My feet are sore."

Onnin gave a curt nod.

Buddy squatted down and groaned. "I'm so stiff."

"You're too young to be stiff."

"How old do you think I am?"

Royah winked. "A hundred and ninety?"

Buddy laughed and stood up. "Waiting on you, big guy."

Onnin had squatted too. He smirked and stood up again, looming over them both.

"I think I'm growing on him, Royah."

Onnin's humor vanished. "I wouldn't go so far."

"Are we ready?" She looked around at her protectors. "Wait. I think I need to change her."

Buddy sniffed. "*Eww*. You definitely do."

"You can't smell her from there. I should make you do it."

Buddy opened his eyes wide. "You'd have to. And you'd need Onnin's help. By the time he made a move, I would run for it."

"Where?"

"Uh..." He pointed in every direction before fingering toward one. "This way!"

Regardless of how she felt about Buddy, he was quite funny and fun to have around. The men waited patiently as Royah changed Emma. While she did, Buddy decided to go through his pockets.

Royah wondered if it was possible to develop feelings for two men at the same time. For some reason, thinking about it made her uncomfortable.

"Done," she exclaimed.

"Good." Buddy placed a hand on the butt of his pistol in its holster. "We're almost there.

17. MELVIN

When had it been since the last time he'd attempted contact? He eyed the radio. Sometimes, he did things so automatically that he scarcely remembered having done them. He could tell it always made Ash anxious.

"Soon."

Even though his mind sometimes betrayed him, he was going to live a long time. Many more years. His sense of purpose kept pace with his age, sped past it even, especially while reading the document. Knowledge kept him young in mind.

Imagining what the journalist described, made it seem as if he were actually there. He wished he could have been able to witness the war firsthand. Not to mention all of the experiments he could have conducted. Especially after the final battle.

The war defined what the planet was today. It made everyone who they were. He was probably the lone person on Home who understood that. He knew what really happened because of the document's existence.

Although Pal may have snuck a peek at it, Melvin took great pride in having the knowledge to himself.

"If anyone deserves such a thing, it is I."

After carefully sliding his prized possession back into the envelope and inside his desk drawer, he shut it. And then shoved it, ensuring it was closed.

He enjoyed reading the document. Not because he forgot details—quite the contrary, he'd practically memorized them—it was because he enjoyed envisioning himself during the war, as if he were present.

The more his eyes soaked in the words, the clearer the circumstances of the period became to him. As far as he could tell, every word was true. The journalist had no reason to embellish. Maybe somewhat, for dramatic purposes. To accentuate the details.

"Who was he really writing it for, though? Himself? A publication? Who did he eventually wish to read it, once he was being hunted?"

Melvin liked to imagine it was written for someone like himself. There had been tremendous conflicts occurring, but all of it was completely out of the journalist's control. He had been a bystander from the beginning.

Being a bystander appealed to Melvin because it was familiar. There were many times when he wasn't in control because of his dependence on others. Unless he was in his lab.

Reading the document allowed him to vicariously live through the journalist and his experiences.

Upon first discovering the document, he was paranoid it might fall into the hands of someone lesser than him. Less deserving. Someone who couldn't appreciate it.

"Those with important business always possess treasures. Or at least something to steal to covet or trade or sell."

Melvin was also afraid that he might be killed while he was above ground and out on the flat. Vulnerable.

No one would be able to conduct his experiments if he were dead. Not the way he could. Not even Ash. No doubt there were many outliers who wanted to kill Melvin. For personal reasons or no reasons at all.

Irrational murderousness was a common mentality for those who dwelled in the east. For Melvin though, he always had reasons to kill.

Melvin even went through the painstaking process of writing copies in his own handwriting, and stashing them in secret hiding places over the flat.

He didn't expect the copies to remain hidden forever. They would eventually be found, but likely not during his lifetime. Not with how well he'd secreted them away.

Even if they were unearthed, it wasn't as if the common emerger possessed the mental perception to comprehend what was written.

Unless, there was someone like himself, a younger version, who found a copy, destined to pursue a course similar to his own.

It was time again. He hadn't made an attempt in hours. He cleared his throat and coughed.

Picking up the mic, he put his thoughts on hold. "This is Melvin, over."

Endless sound of static radio net.

"Go ahead Melvin, over."

Finally!

One of Pal's lead cronies. Melvin recognized his voice but didn't know his name. Not that it mattered. He was the closest to someone who knew something, which was to say they knew anything. "I need supplies, over."

"Supplies for what? Over."

"Supplies, over," he repeated.

There were a few seconds of empty net and he was afraid the crony wasn't going to key his mic again.

"Let me get a pencil and paper."

Melvin took his thumb off the mic so he couldn't be heard. "Of course he doesn't have everything necessary next to the radio where it would be useful. Whenever I contact them—most of the time it's me who needs things—I have a list for them. To write down. The young do not prepare."

"Go ahead and list the supplies, over."

Melvin pressed the mic. "Clamps for post-surgery, bandages for post-surgery, writing utensils—pencils preferably, notepads or sheets of paper—notepads preferably, beakers, a gun—rifle preferably, currency—"

"How much? Over."

Melvin knew he meant how much currency. "A hundred currency, over."

Melvin didn't require any more currency, he had plenty, but demanding the bills, and only spending it when required, was how he'd obtained so much.

He heard scribblings over the net. Whoever answered usually kept their mic pressed. Sometimes Melvin would have to repeat himself multiple times in order for them to get everything right.

To his annoyance, but he was glad to be so patient. He needed to be. Melvin doubted he could control Pal's army, or be able to even put up with them, as he did. That was why Melvin needed to remain in business with Pal.

"Anything else? Over."

"Knockout gas, over."

"Gas or liquid? Over."

Even as an old man with as much patience required, he got angry often. Had he not been clear? "Gas, over." Actually that gave him an idea. He could use both. "Gas *and* liquid, preferably, over."

"Uh, we only have gas currently, over."

Melvin closed his eyes, bared what teeth were still in his mouth, and slowly shook his head, wisps of beard tickling his lips. He rubbed away the itchiness.

Why act as though either are available if you have only one?

"Why are the young so dumb, Ash?"

He'd pestered Ash enough. Ash was busy doing his own work, which consisted of a constant experimentation.

Fortunately, Melvin possessed plenty of both knockout gas and knockout liquid. The concoctions had been used in the past to put soldiers to sleep while traveling long distances.

Likely, the concoctions were left over from space journeys to get them from wherever they began their journey until they reached Home.

It was fitting that Melvin used the knockout concoctions for similar purposes. In a way. Experiments to figuratively journey emergers to a final evolution.

Ah, what do I have to lose? Ash will never divulge my secrets.

"Forcing sleep on their way, considering this planet and its life, entirely, is an experiment. It makes me feel content. Would you like to know why?"

"Anything else? Over."

Melvin held the mic out and away. "Because my experiments began long before I was born, and all of this is for me."

Melvin waited, but Ash only stared. Not even Ash understood his thought processes.

He thumbed the mic. "Nothing else. Is Pal available to speak? Over."

"Negative, over."

"Have him contact me when he arrives. Over and out."

Once the delivery arrived, he needed to decide what to do with the currency. Add to an established pile, or begin a new one?

When Melvin was nothing but a simple emerger like the rest of them, he collected the practically indestructible bills for years, and had gotten quite keen at locating them. But he could always use more.

Even though technically worthless, he used currency's perceived wealth as power. Everyone else seemed to think it was valuable. The knowledge they thought so, was the only thing about currency valuable to him.

The delivery would likely take a while though, as it typically did, and Pal probably wouldn't contact him any time soon either, so Melvin decided he was ready to go above. To the surface, to search as he did each morning. It was his routine and took up most of his day.

Half anyway, before he resumed his experiments. A pang of anger rose up suddenly. But that was only because he could never explain. The experiments probably wouldn't be called so by other scientists. But Melvin was better than them.

"On Earth, they might consider them something else entirely, close to what the outliers do to one another, but it doesn't matter. What is an experiment other than causing an effect resulting in knowledge?"

Ash didn't respond. He stared with the same blank expression he always did. It was not concerning.

As he readied himself, Melvin remembered he would always rather talk than listen anyway.

"I'm going up but I'll be back." Before the elevator doors shut, Melvin said, "Don't go through my things."

18. MELVIN

The solar power of the machinery rose him toward the surface. It took less than a minute.

The elevator could go directly to the surface but he required some strength exercise. The doors opened and he began his climb up the secondary steel ladder—a failsafe if the elevator malfunctioned—to the bright opening.

He always went up before sunrise, before outliers—who hadn't already been inducted into Pal's army, either by recruitment or desperation—stirred.

His objective was to further research the war by any means possible. So often, the path forward was located somewhere in the past. He would search for any new findings, looking for anything to contribute toward invention.

Preferably new food, which so far had been unsuccessful, and hopefully what he typically requested over the net, but finding it for himself.

He wouldn't cancel any orders. That way he would have more. Excess everything was always better and the stashes were a secret between himself and Ash.

But Melvin did look forward to observing the Alien today. It was a common reward after searching. He loved knowing that his lab, his home, the foundation for human ingenuity, and an alien, which existed beyond human ingenuity, were located in such close proximity.

His lab middled the universe.

After searching, he sent updates about a percentage of his progress. For Pal, whenever he got around to it, or for the rare occasions Pal corresponded over the net with Melvin himself.

All Melvin cared about was his work and thankfully there was an incredible amount to do. Realistically, he required multiple average lifetimes to accomplish everything he'd planned.

As he emerged on the surface of Home after climbing the ladder, he felt the same as he always did, but even younger.

But he knew that he was vulnerable out in the open without the control he wielded down in the lab. The wind blew dirt in his face to remind him that he was as unimportant as anyone else up here.

He always wore goggles to spot threats because of where his lab was located, unless the clouds were so thick he could see well enough to remain unnoticed and safe.

There were usually outliers about—who didn't know him or what he was capable of—who would probably revel in descending to the lab and stealing what was down there, destroying everything he'd created in the process.

Besides his mind failing, or him dying, it was Melvin's lone fear.

Sometimes the wind died down in the afternoon but as long as it was active, and it typically was, he wore the goggles until sundown while walking the surface. If he was out of the lab that long. The sun had always been too bright for him.

All there was to see was empty flat anyway, with blurry, faded, jagged mountains in the distance. His eyesight was fine, maybe even better than most, but even he could hardly make them out clearly.

Luckily, the lab's location was where the flat was littered with many relics from the war; empty shells of forgotten technology, skeletal weapons used during battles, and sometimes actual human remains. Bones were resilient. Ash knew that best of all.

Melvin would have preferred to live at this precise location even if there wasn't a lab below and an alien nearby, because there was so much to discover about the era that fascinated him most.

He honestly could never anticipate what he might find. It was an exciting part of his day, other than new knowledge learned by an experiment.

Sometimes, he spent all day inside one of the shattered weapons as he imagined how it functioned, how much damage it was capable of, and how he would operate it if it was still functional.

If the weapon was mentioned in the war document, he imagined what caused its final obliteration. His imagination made him feel young again.

From one of his experiments of logic, he deduced that for years after the first emergers emerged, other battles happened with the same weapons left over from the war.

The weapons must have been somewhat functional for a long time, and the first emergers had figured out how to operate their complexities. But the results were identical consequences, reducing what was left to even further ruins.

Humans destroyed themselves all over again. In all likelihood, civilizations on Home rose up and were reduced multiple times. Though over a short period of years. Decades to them.

Imagining battles between outliers with no training, the frustration and anger and fear, must have been quite the spectacle.

Thin, emaciated, wild-haired, tossing grenades at each other or firing guns or even state of the art howitzers, the ordnance launching toward whoever they perceived as the enemy, reducing what was left to rubble.

No real intelligence active; instead primitive battle instinct driven to destroy. To take. To covet what remained.

"Which is how all humans..."

Melvin threw his head back and laughed, the wind blowing spittle into his long, gray beard, thinking the high pitch of his voice sounded as old as he actually was.

"Ash! You're not up here!"

His laughter eventually subsided. He wondered how he would have fared in battle if he was fighting amongst them, if times were different and he was never fortunate enough to find the lab. It was impossible to know but he suspected he would fight well.

If only he could live as long as he deserved. There was so much more to learn before he could conduct the next evolution of his experiments. And there would be plenty of them. He no longer kept count of the different phases. His discoveries were ever evolving.

"A life unto themselves. I know you hear me, Ash."

Even though Melvin wore goggles, his eyes were closed—and often were when in deep thought—so he opened them.

He'd become lost in thought. Even before he began searching for whatever he would discover today. He realized he was standing as still as a statue. He froze in place while in deep thought more and more the last few years. He wasn't sure why. Almost as if he were in a trance.

Sometimes, he feared it was the result of his age, actually showing signs of being old as he witnessed happening to others. How forgetful they became. Their minds failing in unknowable ways.

But he did his best to push the frightening thought of his great mind failing—which was another fear of his, other than outliers raiding his lab—deep within, where he forced himself not to think about it much.

Not all emergers were killed during those residual battles, obviously, because, aside from what he'd contributed himself, humans were once again slowly repopulating the planet.

Almost everyone heard the stories of how humans had lived before Home, and they'd heard those stories from the humans who'd been old before them.

Human beings, though brittle and easily killed, were quite strong minded and almost always determined to survive. Except everyone needed to eat, to consume to live. Humans wouldn't be repopulating the planet much longer with protein plants dying out.

No food in the coming years was a concern for everyone who lived on this planet. The schematics of the invention of the plants were predetermined. Their expiration was a conundrum, but wouldn't likely affect himself.

It was an obstacle though. Experiments—by him, and Ash

—might demolish such an obstacle. Gain trust with common emergers.

But the worry dwelled deep, where lesser worries resided in his mind, like his mind eventually failing.

Except solving the problem would help others. Inadvertently help him gain more power. Power over Pal.

19. MELVIN

The imperceptible churn of time beneath the surface of Home was always surfacing something buried. Typically guns and currency but also the occasional priceless find.

The scoutbike was purposefully hidden between remnants of artillery launchers, massive instruments of war made of metal that once played the music of explosions and death. It seemed the launchers were hit with artillery because they'd been blown to pieces.

The fragments hid his vehicle from view well, but they also gave him ample opportunities to spot any new discoveries he may have missed.

Even if someone knew where his scoutbike was located, they likely would have trouble spotting it. His ability to hide it was the only reason there was still a scoutbike in his possession.

Climbing onto the comfortable seat, it squished down even under *his* minimal weight. He turned the ignition lever.

The scoutbike jolted to life, sending out a quiet hum of vibration barely felt or heard. Just because Melvin was old, didn't mean he didn't enjoy driving fast.

After speeding in the opposite direction—from yesterday—for long enough and not seeing anything of interest, he took a break at his favorite spot.

He sat on his scoutbike with his binoculars in hand. Through the magnification, he spotted something very, very interesting.

"Ash, do you see them too?"

There were three people heading toward the Alien. It looked as if they were heading directly for it. They were going there on purpose.

He licked his chapped lips, which stung, tasting blood, and pulled his darkly tinted goggles down to his neck. He spied through the binoculars again to see them clearly. Hoping it wasn't his imagination.

It was him. The Loki.

Unmistakable. He was far taller than the other two. Melvin couldn't believe it. He'd hoped to cross paths with him, without seeking him out on purpose, for decades. The Loki was one of the rare experiments Melvin didn't interfere with. Not after Orthal.

Even though he desperately wanted to. But somehow he knew this day would come. Ash told him so.

Pivoting to adjust his view, and strengthening the magnification, he saw that the red-haired female was quite beautiful. She kept looking up at the Loki, and she was holding something.

An infant. She was holding a baby.

Melvin felt decades melt away. He was half his age in an instant.

"I'm not imagining this. This is real. This is real! I didn't believe you, Ash. Not at the time. But now I do. You were so right. My lucky day! Our lucky day!"

Melvin clasped a hand over his mouth, silencing the elation spilling out by accident. They likely couldn't hear him at this distance.

Except the man who intrigued him most, might be able to. He was one of the few who had escaped the experiment in Orthal.

Not even Melvin knew how many of them were still alive. Some of them definitely had escaped, proven because of how many disappearances occurred east of Easto. Along with the frightening tales of what became of the missing.

Although he never sought any of them out, especially the man who was the last of his kind—by surgery—Melvin always hoped to cross paths with them again, so that the next phase would begin naturally.

Melvin obsessed about what the experience—which had been one of his ambitious experiments back then—would do to a man. He was almost positive no woman had survived.

And think, the experiment in Orthal began with the discovery of a certain and highly important document. An anonymous account documenting the war.

He must hurry. He didn't have much time. They wouldn't remain near the Alien for long. He always kept knockout liquid in a side compartment attached to his scoutbike, if a situation like it arose. If he could get them to listen long enough, they were doomed. Even the Loki.

But even if they didn't go along with his plan, fall for the initial phase of his ruse, and he was forced to take things farther, in the end he would use the same method he did when transporting large war relics; the solar wench attached to the elevator.

He yanked out his portable radio, the one attached to the scoutbike for such rare occasions. His hand was trembling with excitement and he laughed. Then he scoffed.

It would all be for nothing if this attempt failed. He desperately needed someone to respond right now and follow through with his demands. Hopefully, he wouldn't have to wait this time.

If the initial part of the plan quickly forming in his mind didn't work, then the entire plan would fail. He'd been waiting for this day his entire life. Everything he planned, plotted, and pontificated about was about to evolve.

"I will implement our findings, Ash. I'll discover a way to invent from human past, food much better than those disgusting plants, for myself, and others, and also reinvent life in the form of what was meant to be."

With plants, emergers aplenty, and the lone direct descendant of the soldiers from long ago to experiment on, he would have enough genetic material to begin the process of creating life he approved of.

"New life will invent new lifeforms. Maintain course of the natural progression of mankind, which is to advance progress. On and on and on. With an army of my own, we will be the leaders of Home. Pal, if he's still alive, will work for us."

Melvin took a moment to marvel at his own intellect. What he was about to do will be so substantial that it will cause others to write about him.

The guise of working for Pal was suitable at the moment. But similar to other business relationships, they often run their course, and the current experiment will change everything.

It will edge him closer to his destiny, will begin a new civilization, and those who call him a mad scientist behind his back, something he detested, will tremble with fear.

And to accomplish all of that, the only thing he required was one of those idiots to pick up on the other end of the net.

He squeezed the mic. "This is Melvin, over."

20. ROYAH

It wasn't like Buddy to be quiet. Even though Royah was sure Onnin preferred silence, there had been too much for her, and she got curious.

"You doing all right?"

"Sure." Buddy cleared his throat. "Why wouldn't I be?"

Royah adjusted Emma. "You're normally so chatty."

"Want me to hold her?" Onnin said.

"Just a little longer."

Onnin's mouth was deep inside all his dark beard but it looked like it turned upward. Another grin? Almost. She didn't want to accuse him of it. He'd probably deny it.

"I suppose you're right," Buddy said. "I've been thinking about those people."

"Who we killed?"

"No. Who *we* killed. Me and him."

"Right. You ever need to do that before?"

"Yeah."

"You can talk about it if you want. It might help."

Buddy nodded knowingly. "It's difficult to end a life. Not actually doing it, especially when they're trying to kill you, but dealing with it. Afterward. I don't think anyone is born bad. They become that way. And who's to say what bad is?"

"Bad is willing to kill unprovoked and for selfish reasons," Onnin said in his deep voice. "We did the right thing."

"For us," Buddy said. "I know we did. But why do I feel bad about doing it?"

"Because you're a good guy. And a great shot. Being great has its downfalls."

"Thanks, big guy."

"You're both good men. Neither of you are bad. But I understand how you feel, Buddy."

Royah was about to open up to these men and knew it was because she finally trusted them completely. Now she was certain she could trust other men, just as she trusted her dad when he was alive.

"I encountered bad men before."

Onnin eyed her.

"Really bad men. And I have to live with what they did to me."

Royah glanced at them, hoping she wouldn't see them alarmed, but that was not the case. Her intent was to open up to them, not get sympathy.

Onnin looked as if he were ready to fight somebody right now, and Buddy looked as angry as Onnin did.

"It was years ago that I got myself—"

Onnin held a massive hand up. "You didn't get yourself into anything." His tone conveyed the truth.

Royah got teary eyed. "No, of course not."

She needed to talk about it. She hadn't known Buddy and Onnin as well as others she had during her life, or for nearly as long, and she wasn't sure why it had to be now, but they were her friends. Real friends were understanding.

"You don't have to say anymore," Buddy said. "We know enough already."

"I think I need to."

Royah waited. Both men would listen.

"When bad things happened. To me. Those who were responsible, they weren't always like that, right? I mean how could they be? Look at little Emma here. At what point did they turn into people who could do such shocking things?"

Both her friends were stunned silent. She sensed their frustration and helplessness at not being able to prevent her from having gone through such trauma.

She almost regretted revealing such painful memories from her past when she remembered how she was always trying to get them, and others, to talk to her about who they were and where they'd been. And what they'd experienced.

Always trying to get others to open up was probably because deep down, it was what she needed to do herself. Although uncomfortable, she felt comfortable enough to tell her new friends about her worst experience. And now she felt even closer to them than she did before.

"I'm sorry for what happened to you." Onnin's gravelly voice was quiet now but she could still hear him. "Some are born with evil in them. It spreads and strengthens with each act of anger or violence. Becoming easier. Some learn how to hide it. But it's always there under the surface. If you know what to look for."

21. ROYAH

Royah tried to read into what Onnin had said, and Buddy was likely doing the same thing.

Sensing their questions, Onnin's massive chest heaved up and down. "I've done terrible things. Evil is in me because of it. Except I'm in control. It allows me to recognize evil in others, which is why I know for certain both of you are good."

Royah flashed a glance at Buddy, and he shot her the same stunned look. But then he forced a grin.

"You're not the only one who can sense things about people," Buddy said. "You're good too."

The shadow of a cloud darkened Onnin's face briefly and lingered. "Not always."

"Well, I'm sure you had your reasons," Buddy said. "In the future, if I hear emergers telling those untrue stories about you, I'll set them straight."

Onnin was about to object.

"And if they argue with me, I'll let my gun do the talking."

Onnin grinned. "That won't be necessary. I can fight my own battles. But thank you."

"You're welcome." Buddy turned to Royah. "I am also sorry for what happened to you. You're a good woman. A good person. If I could go back in time and protect you, I would. And I'd kill every last one of them before they ever laid a hand on you."

Buddy's mouth hung open. He wanted to say more. He was searching for the right words but couldn't seem to find them. But he'd said enough. Both of them had.

Said enough, so now Onnin didn't look at Buddy the same way he had upon first meeting him. He no longer regarded him as a rival, or as a potential enemy, but as an ally.

It was obvious how all three regarded one another; they were a team.

Royah was suddenly uncomfortable with being compelled to open up about her worse experiences. Whatever her intent had been, whatever it was she'd been meaning to get across to them, it happened.

Exhaling, feeling much better, she rubbed Emma's head, and said, "Thank you. Thank you both for listening."

They continued on. Mainly the ground was flat, but occasionally cracks and depressions showed in the land.

When peeked into, the chasms stretched deep below the surface, reaching down toward an infinity of darkness. So often, Home's landscape was as uneven as the levels of its danger.

Everyone watched their step. And everyone watched one another's too. There were no protein plants growing in the area for some reason, reminding Royah of what her mom said about them; they weren't growing as much as they used to.

The possible prevention of protein plants dying out, or at least discovering how and why, was a pillar of the quest.

Royah glanced up, and what she saw held her gaze. One of the mountains looked to be much closer than the others.

Rare that such a mountain was well in view, it also struck Royah as odd. It actually looked like the shape of a man. She also thought it was curious that a rock could look alive.

Similar to how she could somehow make out faces and other familiar shapes in clouds—she always suspected they were animals from Earth, what she'd never seen before but mysteriously recognized—until the clouds drooped, or drifted, changing forever.

The thought always made her sad for some reason, the idea of what was, would never be again, and she suddenly missed her mom very much. She actually felt homesick for the first time since she'd left Westo.

Homesick for a dangerous town she lived in and where awful things happened to her. She shivered. She didn't understand why she felt that way. It didn't make sense.

Maybe because Westo was familiar. Everything lying ahead was not.

The mountain in the shape of a man seemed to be moving ever so slightly, almost vibrating.

Royah squinted. "That's no mountain."

"Nope," Buddy said.

"What is it?"

"The Alien." Buddy walked ahead of them. "Everyone wants to know what caused the destruction on this planet." He pointed up. "It was that thing."

22. YOHIRO

Four men approached as he and his father were about to turn in for the night. Separating, they surrounded them before Yohiro could get Ito inside the safety of their house. The wooden steps were right there but it was a risk to open the door. They might get in.

Yohiro was self-assured because of what he'd done to Bloomfeld and his deputies. It changed the town. Sudden violence—most would consider to be extreme in nature—often caused a ripple effect.

But Yohiro was still taken off guard. He believed the peace would have lasted longer. Not be challenged so soon. Maybe not at all. It was a lesson he would not forget.

Whatever is done, expect the same in return, he thought.

Except the outliers weren't trained. He identified that within a fraction of a second. Yohiro was trained, though. By a robot.

"Think you can just come in and make it the way you want?"

The one who spoke, looked as if he'd gone without sleep for days, and although the other three weren't as disheveled as those who typically frequented the outskirts of town, all of them were unruly.

They resembled the deputies Yohiro had killed, but he didn't recognize any of these ones. Maybe new to town? They also must have been working for Bloomfeld, stealing for him, but they hadn't started making the rounds yet.

Or at least not enough to be recognizable on this side of town. They were probably even called deputies by Bloomfeld, and thought of themselves as such, but a title is just a word. Thieving outliers was more apt.

And outliers like them didn't belong in Easto. Not anymore. Not ever again.

Deciding on displaying coolness instead of apprehension, Yohiro looked at Ito who was just ahead of him. "Please go inside, Father."

Ito almost objected but clearly remembered what his son was capable of. He did as Yohiro asked, rushing up the stairs and opening the front door, and quickly shutting it behind him.

"*Please,* he says."

The others laughed.

Now that his father was safely inside, Yohiro could do as he wished, and he felt the rush of anticipation.

Ito would be out of sight in case there was shooting, but also holding a gun if his involvement was necessary. His father was always ready to retrieve the pistol from where it was hidden. Just in case an altercation such as this occurred at their house, all the while hopeful it would not.

Ito was the newly elected overseer, and he'd obeyed the laws of Easto, even obeyed someone as corrupt as Bloomfeld when he was in charge. Except for his gun law.

The pistol was made to be even more accessible lately. Yohiro and his father agreed that if there was one man in town who might require a gun for a desperate situation, it would be the overseer.

And if anyone could handle the responsibility of owning a gun in town, it was Ito. Even so, Yohiro knew action by his father wouldn't be necessary this evening. He didn't have time to explain.

"You were Bloomfeld's outliers."

"*Outliers*? Did you hear him?"

"I heard."

"Me too."

Yohiro wanted to rile the haggard men up before the fight. It made sense Bloomfeld would have had multiple groups of so called deputies handling different areas of town. And obviously, not all of them showed themselves on every street. Easto was rather large.

Both Yohiro and Ito were much more familiar with its streets since Ito became overseer, but even they hadn't met everyone in town.

The men didn't even glance in the direction of the front door. They didn't care who lived there or who it belonged to. They were focused on Yohiro. Intent to fight, staring with frustration, and hate. They were there to kill him.

It was revenge they were after. Yohiro knew it because if he were them, he would want the same thing. Difficult not to think so when staring at the person responsible for taking away their living.

He decided to feign confusion anyway. "What do you want?"

"Justice."

"Justice was done."

"A crime was done, you mean. We want what's coming to us."

Yohiro's gaze narrowed. "You will."

They should have pulled their guns already. Yohiro yanked out his sword. His father was probably waiting to open the door, which was now slightly ajar—Yohiro heard it open behind him—and ready to shoot the pistol he no doubt held ready.

But he held off. After witnessing what Yohiro did in the store, Ito obviously believed his son could handle himself. Yohiro took it as a compliment. The men weren't expecting Yohiro to react so quickly, so they hadn't reacted.

They clearly didn't understand what he was capable of. Even though they certainly heard about him. If they were dense enough to underestimate who they were dealing with, then it justified their fate.

If they truly knew the danger they were in, they would have avoided the altercation altogether. Or shot at him from a distance.

"You're outnumbered—"

In the blink of an eye, Yohiro chopped off his arm. His last word rose into a scream and he fell against the man closest to him, splashing hot blood all over his face and body.

Yohiro slashed at the other man's torso, taking advantage of him being temporarily blinded by blood, opening deep gashes exposing shiny guts. Both men fell to the ground and died.

Two left; one of them pulled a pistol and shot it. Yohiro anticipated and dove over the fence. The blast briefly looked as bright as the sun but it missed him.

The man pulled the trigger three more times, each sizzle splintering not only the wooden fence but also the evening's silence, and leaving a blackened smoking residue.

Yohiro remained out of view, his eyes clamped shut. He was about to stand up but he was waiting for the bright blur to fade from his vision.

"Is he dead?"

"I think I nicked him. What are you going to do now?" he yelled. "I've got open ground. You don't. Come on out!"

Having lost sight of him, the men didn't realize that Yohiro had already climbed up onto the short roof of the house next door and was looking down on them. He watched as the man doing the talking aimed his gun where he believed Yohiro was still crouched.

Yohiro leapt down silently, closing the distance over the unobstructed ground the pistol wielder believed he controlled.

As he did, he rolled and swung his sword, snagging a neck with it, a frightened look on the face of the head attached, feeling the blade slide into flesh and hit bone.

Yanking quickly to face the last of them, Yohiro thrust the tip of the sword through his eye, and his expression was frozen by death before falling backward.

As he fell to the dirt, the one with the neck wound was still upright. He choked and dropped the pistol. He'd been the one shooting at Yohiro. His hands were at the gash, trying to stop the blood from pouring out.

As if there was a chance to save himself.

When he collapsed, he kept his eyes on Yohiro, even after he died. Yohiro gladly moved out of view, wiped the bloody blade in the crook of his robed arm until it was clean, and re-sheathed the sword.

The gunblasts drew people out of their homes, including Ito's team of assistants. They lived across the street. They were who Ito had appointed to help him with overseer duties.

Ito—and Yohiro—decided they were too passive to call them deputies. The term 'deputy' held a negative connotation from Bloomfeld's meanness anyway.

The assistants walked over.

One of them said, "Are you all right?"

His father opened the door and walked out onto the porch. Ito joined the group getting bigger by the minute and hugged his son. Then he motioned for the assistants to remove the dead men from the street.

As Ito instructed them to take them to the morgue, even more people gathered. Word of what happened and gunblasts, especially the lack of them lately, traveled fast. Even in a town as large as Easto.

23. ROYAH

A thing? It looked much more than a thing. More like a *him* to her, but it was difficult to make out what the Alien actually looked like under all the natural buildup—including so much protein plant growth under his chin, it looked like a beard.

But there was definitely a being in there somewhere. There were other hints of life too, other than his actual human-like form, but Royah couldn't have explained it. He was completely still but then not quite.

His skin, if it could be called that, looked wrinkly. Like an old person. Sun warmed it for so long that it blended in with the ground and the rest of the flat. He resembled a wise old man who was busy thinking.

"It's been here for a million years by the looks of him. Don't you think?"

Royah wasn't sure.

Buddy finished his thought. "Probably even longer. Probably eats all the stuff growing off him to survive."

The Alien was covered in dust and dirt and protein plants and other natural growth from sitting in the same position for so long.

Even if Buddy was wrong in his assumptions—there was no way for him to be sure being in his twenties himself—the Alien had been there a long time.

Longer than humans, based on how much he blended in with the mountains surrounding him far in the distance.

It seemed he had legs, and those legs might be able to walk. But he obviously hadn't for a long time. Royah wondered why. She also wondered why she thought of him as a *he*.

"You've heard of it right?"

"Sure I have."

"Ever seen it in person?"

"No."

"Don't go telling people that I don't take you to nice places."

After she laughed, Buddy turned to Onnin. "How about you?"

Onnin nodded.

"Really? What do you think?"

"About what?"

"About anything. Think I'm right in my assumptions?"

"I wasn't there, Buddy."

"Well, me neither, but it makes sense. Right?"

"I don't believe it was responsible for the destruction. I do think you're right about how long it's been here."

"How could one of them have done this?" Royah said. "How would he have done it?"

Buddy shrugged. "Maybe there used to be more of them."

"But why? What was their purpose? And why is he still here? And alone?"

"Hmm." Buddy covered his brow with a hand and peered upward.

"I mean, what's the point of him being here, if all he wanted to do was destroy everything?"

"He—*it* obviously conquered this planet. Now it's ruling it."

Royah liked Buddy and respected him. She was doing her best to understand his perspective. But none of that made sense to her.

She too looked up at the Alien. "He doesn't look like he's ruling. He doesn't look like he's doing anything at all. Except waiting."

"What could it possibly be waiting for?"

"How should I know? If what you've said is true, wouldn't he squash us right now? I mean we're pretty close. If you really thought he was so dangerous, would you allow us, me and Emma, to walk up to him?"

"A valid point, I guess. I don't know. He's dormant or something. A lot of people have ideas about what happened. But I think I'm one of the few who's close to the truth."

Royah held up a hand to block the sun, the one not helping cradling Emma in the carrier on her front, as she gazed upward. "Are you sure? He doesn't look like a threat. Is he even alive? He looks like a statue."

"Oh, he's alive all right." Buddy searched the ground. He bent over and picked up a rock. "I can prove it. Watch."

Buddy threw the rock as high and hard as he could. The Alien was in a sitting position but he was so tall that the rock clipped the lower part of his ankle. The rock bounced off him with a chirp.

The Alien didn't move.

Then again, how did she react when small specks of dirt bounced off her legs when the wind picked up? Hardly at all.

Buddy turned to them. "See?"

"See what?"

"He flinched."

"No, he didn't."

"Well, maybe not this time, but I've seen him move before. He hasn't in a long time though."

"But you were here when he did?"

"Yeah."

"He walked?"

"No."

"What did he do?"

"Um, I don't know. I don't remember. It just looks alive to me."

"Like he does now? How someone alive seems alive, even when they're holding still?"

"Exactly."

"If he's responsible for nearly annihilating all the—" Royah suddenly pointed. "Wow! He blinked!"

"Oh yeah, right. I forgot. That's all it does though. Doesn't even block when you throw stuff at it either. Know why?" Buddy cupped his hands to the side of his mouth. "You won't do anything because you feel so guilty, you coward!"

The Alien didn't even blink.

"Are you sure it's wise to yell at him?"

Onnin chortled.

Buddy wiped spittle from his mouth. "It knows what it did."

The Alien continued to stare out at the horizon as if in a state of remembrance, and Royah suspected Buddy was grasping for any explanation.

Answers helped people understand, feel safe even, and for Buddy the Alien was something to blame and also take out his frustration. Even though what happened to previous generations hadn't happened to him.

Buddy, like the rest of the emergers, was forced to deal with the aftermath of the war. The time after war could never be ideal living circumstances. Maybe there were even multiple wars considering the destruction of the planet.

Buddy's frustration didn't have roots in her opinion, but she wouldn't continue to disagree with him.

The Alien's presence was mysterious, though. And confusing. Fascinating, too. What was he really? Where did he come from? Why was he here? And why did he remain on Home? If he wasn't involved in the war, then what had he been doing while it was happening?

Perhaps the rest of his species left him behind. Perhaps the mystery of his presence held more secrets than any of them could fathom. He was a being, but everything he was born from and for was lost to time.

No matter the answers, she hoped Buddy was wrong. The last thing this planet needed was another enemy to face. Also, more death and destruction.

"It's too big and looks so powerful that it must have been responsible." Buddy wouldn't give up on trying to convince them.

"I understand why you think so, but you weren't alive back then."

"It's not like I made it up. Others told me too. I choose to believe."

"Why?"

"It makes sense."

"But how do they know? They weren't alive then either. Maybe this is his planet. Maybe it belonged to him before we even got here. Ever think of that?"

"I can sense strength. Can't you?"

"I'm not sure why that's relevant."

Buddy motioned to Onnin. "Of course you do."

She felt herself blush. Thankfully, Onnin was busy gazing up at the Alien and didn't react to Buddy's remark.

"Probably, one of the rare times you've ever looked up at somebody?"

Onnin turned toward Royah and nodded.

"It's not a somebody," Buddy said, "it's a thing."

"I can think of it how I like."

Buddy scoffed. She wasn't sure if she could sense strength, as Buddy suggested. Maybe. One thing she could definitely sense was how alive the Alien was even though he was immobile. Similar to when old people looked at her when she was a little girl or how her mom did.

They weren't saying anything, but they were clearly thinking all kinds of things. Comparing how they were at the same age, recognizing mistakes she would one day make, or having noticed the accomplishments already under her belt. Who knew?

Probably the same way she looked at Emma. Worrying about her even though she'd cared for her for a short time, but also wondering what lay ahead in her future.

"And then there's me, of course."

Royah looked over at Buddy. "Hmm?"

"What I was saying before. You can obviously sense strength. Onnin isn't the only man present. How I'm strong too. Oh, never mind."

"Your will is strong," Onnin said. "We both sense it. Don't we?"

She dipped her head toward Buddy. "Of course."

Buddy grinned. "Thanks for saying so, big guy."

Onnin cleared his throat, which sounded more like a grunt.

The longer Royah stared, the longer she was able to take in what she was seeing. Both men seemed to be as curious as she was, so they were there for quite a while. Understandable, since they'd deviated from their path to come there.

The Alien's lack of movement reminded Royah of what she'd learned about trees and plants on Earth, how they were constantly growing; but because they grew so slowly, it was impossible to see.

Large things still moved but sometimes they didn't move as fast as the dominant species on a planet. It was probably because they didn't have enemies.

Royah noticed Onnin adjust his stance out of the corner of her eye. She swiveled her gaze to what drew his attention.

There was something coming toward them at ground level, beyond the Alien. Many somethings.

Onnin already aimed his rifle. "Outliers."

24. ROYAH

"Buddy, will you hand me my binoculars?" Royah turned away from him. "They should be just inside."

Buddy opened the flap of her backpack, dug around without looking, couldn't find it, lifted the flap, peeked inside, grabbed the binoculars, and handed them to her.

"Thank you."

The distance shimmered from the sun, and dust billowed everywhere. There was a dust storm. Except this one had been created by emergers.

Buddy cupped his hands over his eyes. "There's a lot of them, isn't there?"

"Yes."

"And out of nowhere. What are they doing here?"

"Not to admire the Alien," Onnin grumbled.

There must have been hundreds of them emerging from the curtains of dirt and dust in the distance, as if they would never end. They were definitely heading in their direction, toward the Alien.

Buddy pulled his pistol. "They're going to see us."

"They already have. Or they know about us somehow." Onnin moved his rifle. "Some are on scoutbikes ahead of the others."

Royah lowered her binoculars, and as she did Onnin snapped his head to the side, then swung his rifle and aimed behind them.

An old man with skinny arms threw his hands up. "Don't shoot! Don't shoot."

Onnin's aim didn't falter. He kept it on the stranger. The old man was wearing light clothing meant to block the sun but also to stay cool. He wore no armor. Curious.

He seemed frail, was short, and his skin was dark from too much sun exposure. He had a long gray beard. He also wore strange, oversized goggles, reminding Royah of a child wearing something a few sizes too big.

Because of Onnin's agitation, Buddy aimed his pistol at him too.

"I'm not dangerous!"

It was almost comical the way the old emerger held his hands up in the air. Still, Onnin did not lower his rifle.

Now Buddy's finger was on the trigger. "Where did you come from?"

"I'm so glad I ran across someone. They're after me. I hope I didn't lead them here. I think I did, though. I'm sorry. I know a safe place. It's where I hide. It's nearby. Follow me. If they get us, they'll kill us."

Royah put the strap dangling from the binoculars over her head. There was something about the old man that seemed off. Was he confused? Maybe his mind was sick. He was very old, after all. "Is this place you speak of a town?"

"Where we're going? I don't have time for this! *We* don't have time for this! I can explain everything later."

Onnin kept his rifle aimed at the old man but he turned his head to view the distance. The army was closing in. Then he glanced at Royah.

"It'll be night soon. Follow me now or I leave you behind. They aren't interested in taking prisoners."

"We have a baby." Royah heard her voice tremble.

"I noticed. Where I'll take you, you'll be safe. I promise. It isn't far. But we must hurry!"

Trust a stranger they just met, or face an army of outliers headed their way?

Onnin was no one to be taken lightly, even by an army, but he was only one man. If defeated...

They would surely kill them, take everything they carried, including Emma. Royah hated to think anyone would harm a baby.

Following the frail old man was the smarter choice. She hoped.

Buddy seemed to think so. He lowered his pistol.

Onnin relaxed his grip on his rifle and lowered it too. “Anyone else at this hiding place?”

“My partner, Ash. But don’t worry, he’s harmless.”

25. YOHIRO

A man neither of them recognized, entered the store as it was about to close for the day with deliberation.

Ito greeted him as he did all customers, but then kept a watchful eye on him. Not because he looked like an outlier or a thief. On the contrary, he exuded strength, and that was a trait not seen every day. He might be an overseer from a nearby town.

His father's wariness put Yohiro on edge, and he watched the man carefully, ready for what transpired the other day to happen again. The peace thought to be established after Bloomfeld's death, had been short lived.

Strangers could be a threat. This man would be treated no differently.

Bloomfeld had appeared in Easto the same way, unexpectedly, and those who'd been in charge naïvely trusted him.

The newcomer had a medium build, short dark hair, and a friendly face. For some reason, it was his appearance that caused Yohiro to be suspicious.

He reminded Yohiro of dads standing with their families and smiling in those paper ads—the ones some people paid a lot of currency for, as a collector's item—advertising a family vacation on Earth.

His hair looked trimmed recently and his stubbly beard groomed also. He looked nothing like the outliers who often wandered in from beyond the outskirts of Easto.

In contrast, he wore a vest and pants. What a soldier wore, with large pockets with room for armored plating. It must have been left over from the war. Except it was in terrific condition.

The color of the uniform was the same as protein plants,

green, and it looked designed in a way to blend in with the terrain. Camouflage.

There were also places to attach things on, like grenades or guns or knives, except he looked to be unarmed.

His eyes were active over the store, even though he behaved as if he'd been there before. He seemed to be intent on taking everything in within sight, within seconds before he planned to speak.

He gave a respectful nod toward Ito, who was standing behind the counter, when his scanning crossed Yohiro and focused on him directly.

Yohiro realized the stranger was doing the same thing he was, searching for potential danger. The stranger stood at an angle, allowing him to keep an eye not only on Ito, but also Yohiro.

Stories of Yohiro and his skills with a sword might have reached his ears, but then maybe he was smart enough not to underestimate anyone he didn't know, as Yohiro did.

After seeming to commit the store to memory, he again turned to Ito, smiled broadly—showing a lot of white teeth—and walked toward him, extending a hand.

His smile made Yohiro want to trust him, but his eyes looked like he'd seen a hundred battles, making Yohiro wary of first impressions.

"Hello." The stranger shook his father's hand with an enthusiastic grip. "I'm Pal."

"Overseer Ito."

"It's nice to meet you."

"You as well."

If Pal offered to shake Yohiro's hand, he wasn't about to reciprocate. Though he looked nothing like the men Yohiro used his sword against, Yohiro stared at the stranger in his father's store wondering if he were the threat he sensed him to be.

Pal's face was younger than those men, and also his father. He seemed kind, was friendly, but Yohiro didn't doubt the violent history within Pal's eyes. His posture reminded Yohiro of the warriors he read about in his books.

No matter how things went in the next few minutes, he would be ready. His sword was out of sight. Pal likely commanded followers to remain nearby to—

"You won't be needing that." Pal eyed the shadow of the room where Yohiro's sword had been placed.

Though shocked, Yohiro said nothing.

"How may I help you?" Ito said.

Pal smirked at Yohiro, tilted his head and then shifted his attention back to Ito. "I'm a local businessman such as yourself, and I'm afraid to admit I've recently made a poor investment."

"We've all been there."

"Nice of you to say so."

"Which investment are you referring to?"

"Bloomfeld."

Seeing his father shake Pal's hand earlier and his first words had relaxed Yohiro somewhat, but the mention of any association to the former overseer made him inadvertently take a sidestep toward his sword.

To convey how the conversation would go if they continued to dislike what Pal said.

His movement wasn't lost on Pal. He held up his hands. "I know what you're thinking—"

"You do not," Yohiro interrupted. "And I do not have my father's temperament. Choose your words carefully."

Pal gave him a respectful nod. "You're wondering if I'm a villain like he was and you'll kill me too, if you believe me to be a threat."

Pal lowered his hands and waited. He did not seem to be afraid. He seemed to be on their side. Probably acting, for reasons neither him, nor his father, understood. They didn't know the man.

"Go on," Ito said.

Pal scratched the top of his head and seemed to be aware of the dangerous predicament he was in. "Bloomfeld was the opposite of who I wanted to lead Easto. And I was unaware of how corrupt he was."

"He worked for you?"

Pal pursed his lips thoughtfully. His facial expressions were animated and of course he was aware that he was being scrutinized. How one false move could make him as dead as Bloomfeld and his deputies. He seemed to be behaving how they hoped someone in his position would.

"I'm embarrassed to say so, but yes, he did. I was hoping for stability, but Bloomfeld made Easto even more chaotic. Consistency is important for citizens. Everyone feels vulnerable while out on the flat, but the flat is unavoidable. But towns are the most consistent intervals on the flat, and them remaining upright is paramount. Wouldn't you both agree?"

"Why choose Bloomfeld?"

His father asked the question Yohiro was thinking.

"I didn't know him well but people followed him. So I thought he would follow my lead. Not everyone works out, I'm afraid. I've been to Easto before, but it was years ago. Then I heard how dangerous it became. I asked some of my men if they would clean it up. I couldn't do it myself. I have too much to oversee, so when Bloomfeld volunteered, the job was his. I couldn't know how badly he would foul things up. In a way, no, *I am* responsible for what happened. It's why I'm here. To fix things."

"Things no longer need fixing," Ito said. "We've done it ourselves."

Pal smiled. "Making my amends much easier."

Upon inspection, Yohiro saw impressions of metal plates, the outline of them, pressing from inside Pal's camouflaged uniform. He was indeed wearing armor. Pal was ready to, and willing, to be shot at.

Was he ready for a sword slash, though?

Pal was busy talking to his father but also carefully watching Yohiro out of the corner of his eye. He remained in a position to view them both. He must have something up his sleeve, if the meeting went as south as Southo.

Yohiro wondered how many men were waiting outside. Or just outside town.

"I'm glad you brought up assuming responsibility. I see something in you, Ito, a similarity between you and I. Whenever something needs fixing, even if it might be humiliating, I'm willing to sacrifice, whether it be my time or even my life, if it's important enough."

"Like a soldier."

"And a parent."

"You have children?"

"No, but I remember being young, and my mother believed in me." He winked at Yohiro. "She told me that I was capable of changing the planet if my will was strong enough. It just depended on how determined I was. And how well I adapted when things don't go according to plan."

Pal looked over at Yohiro, stared at him for a few seconds, then turned his back on him, focusing on Ito.

"And what is it you want?"

"Stability for Home. How often do you fear outliers wandering into town to disrupt what you've established here, especially after what happened?" He didn't wait for Ito to answer. "I want progress. I want something more than what we have, what we've been left with. This isn't how humans are supposed to live. We're supposed to thrive, not just survive."

"We're doing all right."

"Yes. But how long until outliers show up and try to take this town again, maybe people worse than Bloomfeld."

"You're the one who hired him."

"He was a mistake. I've made many. I'm sure you have too. Everyone has. And I'm sure I'll make more. But I'm doing something here. Trying to live up to what my mother hoped for me before she died."

"How did she die?"

Pal hesitated as if it were painful to remember. "She got caught in the middle of a gunfight. Then they knew I was alone and wanted what we owned, so they wanted me dead. But I escaped."

"No father while growing up?"

"He left us long before then. I don't even remember him. Only what my mother told me about him."

"I'm sorry."

"Eventually, and it took a while, I realized those responsible were just emergers. Not good, not bad, just doing what they had to in order to survive. Similar to myself. They didn't know any better because they weren't taught any different. I will teach emergers to understand what human beings are capable of to reach their potential. Teach them the right way."

"Which is?"

"Better than our present. I have to be honest, I never thought I would get this far, thought I'd get myself killed like my mother did long ago; yet with everything I've done, mistakes and successes, I simply walked into your town as if I weren't a threat."

"Are you?"

"Anyone can be. My point is, people trust me, and I know people. Not everyone can reach their potential but many try. Outliers aren't brainless monsters to be feared. Some are, but many are good enough to have the potential to be better. I intend on giving anyone an opportunity. Unless they prove otherwise."

"Like Bloomfeld?"

"Exactly."

"Then why threaten us?"

"Threaten. Is that what you think I'm doing?"

"I've lived long enough to know, by your tone, that if you don't approve of our choice, what you haven't presented yet, will cause you to unleash the outliers you speak of, who seem to be under your control."

Pal laughed. "Not all of them! Yet! I like it, Ito. Honesty. I'm in the right place. Leaders have so much to do, to contemplate, to figure out. You have what it takes to be a leader. You and I are going to have many deep conversations. I already know it. But I'm getting ahead of myself. I'm thinking of what I'm going to say before I walk out of here."

"Ambitious." Ito's grin faded. "What was Bloomfeld supposed to do exactly? What were your commands?"

"Instructions. Not commands. He wasn't given any specifically. Run the town and run it right. It was his job to make it stable, not shake down its citizens for extra currency." Pal waited. "I did have an ulterior motive by sending a man like him. Let me ask you something, did you ever wonder why this town wasn't overrun long ago? I mean if the outliers weren't currently busy trying to kill one another."

"The question occurred to us."

"Because I appointed one of their own to run it. I overheard quite a few of them deciding when to invade Easto, but I talked them down. Without a sensible explanation to them, and when I say sensible, I mean straightforward logic, and afraid of one of their own as they were Bloomfeld, how long do you think they're going to wait until fresh conversations lean toward invading and raiding?"

"I don't know."

"Precisely why I'm here. The answer is: soon. All of you have things they desire and I don't want to know another town was reduced to dust because of my inaction, as so many others that thrived but were flooded by desperate emergers and were eventually destroyed. My mother told me all about it, as her father had told her. I'm tired of Home remaining in a constant state of chaos."

"You clearly agree Easto is being run well. And I understand your concerns, but why did you specifically come here, to my store? You haven't mentioned it yet. Tell me what you want."

Yohiro had never been so proud of his father. This was his arena; debating, speaking his mind, and conveying his ideas.

Pal glanced over at Yohiro. Yohiro hoped that he conveyed to Pal how much control he had over the situation. And also would attack him if he must.

"Specifics. I appreciate it. Like many businesses, mine also requires currency. Bloomfeld stopped showing up to pay me my cut. To reiterate, I didn't know he was collecting so much—"

"Stealing," Yohiro interrupted.

Pal stole another look at him, nodding. "Stealing. And far more than what was reasonable." His attention went back to Ito.

"I asked around, the way you're running things *is* reasonable, Ito. What I want, what I'm here for, specifically in your store, is to ask you to take over Bloomfeld's role for me. Running this town, taxing its citizens and paying me a percentage. It will keep the conniving sort at bay."

"My father already took Bloomfeld's role," Yohiro said.

"Exactly," Pal said. "*Took*."

Ito's face hardened. "To the citizens of this town, how would I be any different than Bloomfeld?"

"I understand your suspicion and your hesitance, but most of who everyone fears has joined me. Before you react or give me an answer, please try to understand what I'm doing. What I'm *trying* to do."

"I require further explanation."

"I'm organizing them, bettering them, getting them as far from their origins as possible, in mind, so they can behave as we as humans used to be. When we were at our best as a species. When we were on Earth. It's going to take some time to accomplish it, but time is something we have. We have no choice."

"There are always choices."

"In order to better ourselves, we have only one choice. I'll get into details later. Take the position and you'll get protection. That's a promise. *Organize* means, I have an army made up of the people you fear taking over this town. Think about this: how safe would you feel if there was no one left to attack you?"

"My problem is how could I agree to something that sounds impossible?"

"Because it's necessary. Some of the currency I collect is paid to the outliers and keeps them productive, progressive, and most of all distracted from their own barbaric nature. It gives them a purpose."

"To get them to the point when they're no longer referred to as outliers. Is that the goal?"

"Yes. I'd like you to participate in civilizing and progressing the people of Home. Molding them to reach their potential within the next few centuries. We have the opportunity to evolve the entire planet. You both are responsible, smart, capable, tough men who can surely see my way is better. Everything's been broken since the war, and what I envision *should* be the future. It will be, if I have anything to say about it."

26. YOHIRO

Pal probably remained silent to allow his plan to sink in. He was excited about it, practically trembling. He definitely believed in what he was saying. His father was the one to speak next.

"What if I, if we, refuse?"

Pal exhaled. "Then I'll have no vested interest in Easto. No control. There's no one else I want to assume Bloomfeld's role. I would have to outsource among the outliers. I don't have anyone in mind right now. This isn't a threat, not exactly, but why would I protect a town I'm not collecting currency from? You give your wares away free, Ito?"

Ito shook his head. "Of course not."

A small smile appeared. "I understand you have *assistants*? It's a mistake to call them that. I understand why, the negative connotation related to Bloomfeld, but it's a poor decision. Call them deputies as the former overseer did. The title carries more weight, and you should hold a meeting explaining how he handled things isn't your way. Allow the citizens to elect who will be your deputies, and also allow another election where others may run against you."

"We tried already."

"Try again. If you care about this town as much as I think you do, it's win-win. Either you're unanimously elected again, which I have no doubt you will be, or someone better will have the job."

"Why should I go through all the trouble vying for a position I already have? And don't exactly want."

Pal grinned. "It will absolutely solidify your position as overseer. The people will believe in the rules you set forth, even if they disagree with you. Out of respect. And respect is what is important in how those you lead view you. Also fear, but you saw how fear worked out for Bloomfeld. I'm sorry to tell you this, but those who agreed on you being overseer was a result of the same fear. Of course no one would run against you."

"Ridiculous. No one should fear me."

"Not you," Pal pointed. "Your son."

This man was getting smarter by the minute, Yohiro thought.

Ito visibly objected. "He was only—"

Pal held a hand up. "I understand why he did it. What I'm getting at is, let's say things were different. Someone else killed the overseer on the other side of town, how would you view them if *they* wanted power?"

"It isn't power my father wants," Yohiro said. "Or what made him overseer."

Pal middled himself between them, far enough for a three-way conversation. Again, it was as if it was planned. A strategy. "*We* know that, but how could they? If the situation were reversed, you'd probably go along because you'd be afraid they'd do the same to you if you opposed them. Correct?"

Both Yohiro and his father nodded together.

"Another election will give the people a legitimate choice after the violence. Being a leader is challenging, but I have no doubt you're the best man for the job, Ito. I spoke to folks around town before I even considered coming into this store. When I asked about you, some were nervous, but the rest were not. Anyone who was, I'm sure it was because of what your son did. They believe in you, Ito. Regardless of my instincts about things, they know you better than I do. Except sometimes, I know people better than they know themselves."

Yohiro crossed his arms. "How?"

Pal visibly relaxed. "Put it this way. I see potential. Good or bad."

"You mean beneficial to you or not."

Yohiro got the distinct feeling that Pal wanted something from him as well, not just from his father.

"I've been wrong before. Outliers, unfortunately, even with all of the work I've put into them, are the enemy. But their status in my new world is entirely up to them. Today I control them, guide them, and one day in the future, I hope to consider them all to be allies as opposed to enemies."

Pal was making a lot of sense. His ability to be humble about his mistakes, even if forced to convey his point, was refreshing. Ito seemed to understand his point of view also, but Yohiro still wanted to speak with his father about all of it, but after Pal left.

Whatever Ito decided was the way Yohiro would go too.

"At some point, they will be more civilized. Once it happens, Home will be a safer place to exist because a new foundation will be established. Then a civilized society will pass down their ways to the next generation and then the next. One day, emergers won't have to struggle as much as we all do today. Because of customs as familiar as breathing terraformed air."

"Struggle is what makes us strong," Ito said.

"I couldn't agree more but within normal parameters. There have been instances of savagery far too brutal to be spoken of."

"You mean cannibalism," Yohiro said.

"And worse."

Yohiro wondered what could be worse than cannibalism. "What—"

"Parents who sell their children to them."

It wasn't just battles Yohiro sensed Pal was a part of, it was also a culmination of knowledge, and sometimes knowledge was haunting.

"If I don't do this. If *we* don't do this, then emergers will continue down a path of the same savagery and it will never end. They will never reach the potential that human beings are truly capable of. My purpose is to progress the people of Home to the standards set forth by the humans from Earth, where we are from. We're supposed to behave as those who set foot here in the first place. Not animalistic, diluted shadows."

Ito grinned. "How often do you give this speech?"

"All the time. As often as I can. To anyone who will listen. Will you join me?"

"Yes."

Yohiro got chills. He was so happy his father had agreed. For both of them. It was their destiny.

"Restructuring the leadership in Easto is only the beginning. Together we will rebuild Home. But I have one final request."

"Tell us."

There was trust in his father's voice, when before there was uncertainty.

Pal walked over and stood in front of Yohiro, those wise, battle hardened eyes showing respect. "Your sword."

27. ONNIN

Cast down against his will. Thrown away like garbage. Back at the terrible place. Again. Had he ever left?

The smell of excrement and panicky voices. The dullness of fatigue and confusion and helplessness in the voices of the others.

There seemed to be movement all around him, people trying to get at him like before. He couldn't move very well. As if he were at the bottom of a lake.

Even thinking about moving his arms and legs was a struggle. He would have to grab them, kill them as he did before, start fighting his way out. It would be the only way to survive. He could do it again. He would do it again.

Except a fog was clearing. He was experiencing something he never felt before.

When he opened his eyes, his view went from blurry to less blurry. Then as seconds passed, he felt more normal. But not quite. His senses weren't as amplified. He realized that whatever was wrong with him was in his mind. His brain had been affected.

By what, though?

He was coming out of a dream, which meant he'd been asleep, which also meant he'd been forced unconscious. Going to sleep was always under his control before now. Relief swept over him.

Being in the terrible place again was always a dream. Except now, he was in some other dangerous place. He didn't know where he was, what was happening, or why. For all he knew the current situation was worse.

But being in a worse place than the terrible place was impossible.

His strength was coming back. Slowly. As time went on, his blood burned up whatever had knocked him out. A baby cried.

Emma.

Her diaper needed to be changed. That was what he smelled as he came to, and his mind snapped into focus.

"Roy-*uh*?" His voice sounded strange. Slurred. He shook his head from side to side, seeing if that would help, and wiggled his tongue. It was dry in his mouth. "Roy-*uh*."

"Over here," she said.

Onnin closed his eyes, squeezed them shut, and then opened them again. It helped. More film of grogginess wiped away, the harder he concentrated. Blurry Royah was doing her best to comfort Emma, but she was wailing.

"She's so scared," Buddy said.

Buddy was here. Wherever here was. Onnin was relieved he—they—weren't in the place he feared. Loathed.

Onnin's mind wasn't right. He was dizzy. Someone had done something to him. To all of them probably. Maybe even to Emma. Anger sprouted and grew until it was everywhere inside him.

He cleared his throat and swallowed. His mouth was so dry. "Are you both all right?"

"I'm good," Buddy said. "You must have been given more of whatever they gave us. I was messed up though."

"Royah?"

"I think I'm okay. Are you better?"

"Still foggy but fine. What about Emma?"

"Cranky but doing fine. I need to feed her but I don't have any protein juice. I think it was taken."

They'd been drugged. He couldn't believe he'd allowed them to get themselves into such a situation. It was his fault.

"Where are we?"

"I don't know," Buddy said.

"We were trying to figure it out," Royah said. "Buddy and I woke up about the same time. You last, though."

"Hmm."

"I don't have my rifle. All our—*everything* was taken."

Onnin swiped for his revolver but only felt fatigues. Then he looked around for *his* rifle. Then for his backpack. Royah was right. Someone took their belongings away. Including Royah's necklace.

He didn't want to voice it, but he was having trouble remembering how they got in here in the first place. They were obviously drugged and with something he wasn't familiar with. But how was it possible? How long had they been here?

Sharper eyesight penetrated the gloom. Airborne green mist lingered. It looked as if they were submerged in a lake. Except there was no water.

They seemed to be in some kind of large box. The floor was slick with a wet, powdery residue. Almost oily to the touch. Then he spotted protein plants. Crammed in the corners. What he'd smelled before, besides Emma, when he was dreaming. The familiarity of them.

Except these ones were flattened. Altered. That was probably why it was green everywhere. The fact that there were so many plants meant they'd been tampered with.

The source of their unconsciousness?

Maybe. There was more to it. It was some sort of experiment.

Experiment?

Onnin was once again a frightened young man. "We need to get out of here right now."

"You think so?" Buddy didn't hide his sarcasm.

Slowly Onnin's memory of what happened was coming back.

The Alien...

The outliers...

"What happened to the old man?"

"What old man?" Buddy said. "Oh yeah. Where *did* he go?"

Royah shrugged. "He disappeared."

"Along with our memory."

Onnin hoped it wasn't him. Who he heard about over the years. But how could that frail old man be him?

Onnin never encountered him before, at least not in person, but he heard of what he did to people. They didn't live through what was done to them. As far as he knew, they disappeared and were never heard from again.

If Onnin were anyone else, he'd probably feel chills run up his spine, like his friends Royah and Buddy should, if they knew about him as Onnin did. The stories about him were terrifying. Even the half-truths.

Royah was staring. "You know something, don't you?"

"Enough to understand the danger we're in."

Buddy scoffed. "Do something about it instead of just sitting there!"

"Don't fight, please," Royah said.

Royah jostled fussy Emma in the front pack—at least it hadn't been taken away—but it hardly helped. Emma seemed to sense everyone's alarm too.

Buddy was right though. Onnin was sitting. He tried to stand up but couldn't. He didn't have the energy.

His eyesight was clear enough, so at least he could examine the surroundings better. It was a narrow square room with a high ceiling without a door. At least, not one he could see.

"Do either of you see a way out? I'm sorry. I'm still recovering."

"You likely got more of whatever they, or he, or whoever, drugged us with." Buddy exhaled and peered around. "*I* don't."

Onnin peered up at the ceiling and even though it was dark, it was a likely place for an opening. They were breathing in a confined space, so there must be vents or something. It didn't look as solid as the walls and floor. There were indications of indentations in the dark.

Whoever put them in here was strong enough to lift even Onnin and drop him in. How though?

It wasn't likely, even for the others. Lifting dead weight was heavy. A grown man, or even a group of them, would have trouble lifting Onnin. And that certainly hadn't been accomplished by an old man.

Yet all three of us are in here.

Four, including Emma. The old man probably led them in. Tricked them. But they couldn't remember. There must be a door. There must be a control panel. No doubt located somewhere *outside* the enclosure.

"We were following him from outside, but do either of you remember how we got in here?"

Onnin looked to each of them. Royah shook her head, and so did Buddy. There must be a way out but it was too dim to see. No doubt purposeful. He stared up at the ceiling again. Now he could see better.

Above, amidst the darkness, were wires and tubing. They functioned in ways he didn't understand. He sensed the room was similar to the worst place he'd ever been. People died in here too.

"What are you thinking?"

He glanced over at Buddy. "We're not leaving the same way we came in."

"You see a way out?"

"I'll make one."

"This is my fault."

"No," Onnin said.

"Of course it isn't," Royah said.

"I'm the one who wanted to go see the Alien."

"We all went along. You couldn't know this would happen."

Onnin noticed how frightened Royah was, and how hard she was attempting to hide it. Even Buddy was frazzled. His voice and face were matching his worry.

Onnin's anger gave him energy. He tilted forward and was able to rock onto his feet. And remain upright. Even though he was shaky. It felt as if he hadn't eaten in days. Probably due to what was done to him.

"Not so fast. Save your energy. You're going to need it."

Royah felt along a wall and pointed to a circle of tiny holes, where the distorted voice emitted from. "Who are you?"

The voice from the intercom was robotic, but clearly a man. That man remained silent.

Royah hugged Emma closer, who was quiet for the moment. "He was talking to you," she said to Onnin, before readdressing the mystery voice. "Where are you? Show yourself."

Silence. Some kind of game.

Now on his feet, Onnin peered around the enclosure, giving it a closer inspection. The wall behind Royah looked to be slightly translucent. A large square was visible.

"Royah, will you move to the side?"

Royah did, and Onnin considered ramming it. What stopped him short was the outline of the old man who had claimed to be able to save them from the army of outliers.

He was standing behind the wall, staring in at them. He could probably see them perfectly. Onnin squinted as he could barely make him out.

The old man still wore the same garments, including those strange goggles. His shaggy, gray beard practically took up all of his head. The goggles likely allowed him to see into the gloom.

"Please let us go," Royah pleaded. "We have currency. We can pay you."

The voice from the intercom snickered. *"The guise of worth wasted on those who are incapable of understanding its transparency."*

Royah gasped in confusion, about to say something else. Likely something to antagonize their captor.

"What do you want with us, Mad Scientist?" Onnin growled.

28. ONNIN

The old man didn't respond. But the name clearly agitated him; his head tilted to the side, as was Onnin's intent. Even so, after which, he turned as still as a statue.

Buddy's face scrunched. "Mad *who*?"

Royah's eyes widened. "Oh no."

Buddy stared at the scrawny form outside the enclosure. "You're the old man who lied to us."

"My name is Melvin. It would be wise to address me properly from this moment on."

"Yeah?" Buddy was already defiant. "And if we don't?"

"I've already taken what I require. Your death will be sooner rather than later. I'm debating whether the next phase is of interest. Being impolite will be a factor."

The three of them didn't move a muscle. Terror was all over Royah's face but she was doing her best to hide it.

Buddy looked like he was ready to fight, except he wasn't sure how.

Even Emma was more still than usual, as if sensing how Royah was feeling and was scared herself.

Onnin wanted to punch through the wall and grab Melvin by the throat. Taken what he required. What could that possibly mean? Onnin didn't want to give Melvin any satisfaction but he needed to know.

"Then why are we still alive?"

"Yeah, what did you get from us?" Buddy said.

Buddy was doing his best to be brave, but Onnin knew him well enough to know when he was only feigning it.

Onnin needed to be careful. To not do what he typically did

in a situation like this, especially if he was alone, and lose his temper.

"Blood samples."

"Blood?" Royah looked to Onnin and Buddy. "Even—"

"Yes. Even the infant."

Onnin couldn't see Melvin's mouth moving, but he could see his beard moving up and down. A beard he wanted to grab for grip as he raised his fist back and followed through with all his strength.

He forced an exhale, doing his best to calm himself. His blood was up, and there was only one thing that could happen for him to be normal again. To kill the crazy old man behind all this, the sick one behind the wall, and escape from whatever this place was.

Buddy was disgusted. "Why?"

"Research, of course."

"Stop conversing with him."

Onnin appreciated what Buddy was attempting to do, but it wasn't necessary. They'd made enough decisions together that Onnin knew Buddy understood. Deciding to go on Royah's quest, heading for Slingtown, visiting the Alien.

Now this. Whatever it was. It was definitely orchestrated by a corrupted mind. And Melvin obviously enjoyed the control. Their questions hinted at fear. It was impossible to hide it in their voices. It was surely giving Melvin exactly what he wanted; power over them.

Onnin hated Melvin. Hated people who were like him. Deny him his sick amusement and they might have a better chance of escaping. Though it would be difficult to convey to Royah and Buddy without outright explaining. Their captor would overhear.

"What kind of research?" Buddy said.

Royah slowly shook her head, attempting to convey what Onnin was thinking; engaging with Melvin wasn't smart.

But Buddy mouthed: "It's fine."

No choice but to trust their friend.

"The kind allowing me to build something better. From all of you. To change your genetic integrity if you will, as I did to protein plants. You aren't the first emergers who've woken up in there. I expertly sanitize inside and whoever is in next, won't understand the danger they're in. Until it's too late. As it is for all four of you."

Buddy flushed. "You're insane."

"That isn't how history will remember me."

Onnin held no control over the situation but he needed to get a hold of it and quickly. They were dealing with a monster, and Royah and Buddy were slowly falling apart; Buddy verbally, and Royah visibly.

Royah was actually trembling. Seeing her fear made Onnin even angrier because he couldn't prevent it.

Melvin's head snapped to the side. He was talking to someone, maybe the partner he mentioned, but Onnin couldn't see anyone else. He couldn't hear Melvin clearly when he wasn't speaking through the intercom but his muffled voice rose in pitch and intensity.

As if he were arguing with someone.

The intercom activated and Melvin cleared his throat, cutting in and out like tiny gunblasts. Once again his robotic voice addressed them. *"History will know that it was I who repopulated Home. Taken from those who destroyed it. He is my prize, the rest of you are inconsequential. But still have some use to me."*

"A prize? Who?" Buddy grinned. "Me?"

"Of course not."

"What's he talking about?" Royah said to Onnin.

Onnin was feeling the chills he heard others experienced, creep down his arms.

"This isn't the first time I've tried to retrieve a blood sample from you. I've sent many collectors, but they never returned. You killed them, I suppose."

Yes, Onnin thought.

Buddy looked over at Onnin. "Why do you want *him*?"

Onnin sensed Melvin's anticipation to explain. He practically tittered with excitement as a child would.

"Imagine my surprise when you actually came to me."

"I did nothing of the sort."

"Yet you are here. Were you admiring the Alien as I often do?"

"Admiring it?" Buddy was disgusted. "It destroyed this planet."

Melvin laughed. *"That couldn't be farther from the truth. The large man trapped in the container with you was responsible. And if you knew what I did, it would be better for Home if he were kept there."*

29. ONNIN

"Absurd," Royah said. "The war happened a long time ago. Onnin wasn't even alive then."

Onnin was thinking the same thing himself. There was no telling if Melvin's intent was to deliver the truth or simply add to what already became a slow torture of words.

The situation made him want to punch through the wall, grab Melvin by the throat, and squeeze until he was dead. Then they could all escape and put this place behind them.

"Huh?" Royah said. "I'm talking to you, Melvin."

Melvin was silent. He was simply observing them from behind the—surely transparent, to him—wall.

"He's just messing with us," Buddy said, his anger coming through. "To turn us against each other."

The place and the crazed man in charge of it was putting them behind on their quest, and unless they figured something out, and fast, it might be the end of their lives.

The intercom squawked. *"I must forgive your lack of knowledge. But also, I misspoke. You see, he has a direct bloodline to those who began the destroying of Home."*

"How do you know?" Royah said to the shadowy figure.

Silence again. Enjoying his control.

"Do you have any idea what he means?" Royah said to Onnin, since Melvin wouldn't answer.

"No."

"He's crazy," Buddy said. "It's obvious. But he seems to think he can clone Onnin. Create an army from him."

"There's a bright one." The slight revelation of information was like permission for Melvin to explain his deranged rhetoric.

"Lokis arrived after the colonists, who were the first humans on this planet. Onnin is one of them."

"What's a Loki?" Buddy said.

"A nickname the soldiers gave themselves. Not unlike what some call me in terms of its inaccuracy."

"So the Alien wasn't involved?"

"Not as bright as I thought. Shall I go on? Lokis differed from the colonists, who were base humans, in wondrous ways. By their agility, size, and mental acuity. Their purpose was also different. Over time the war began."

"You're skipping over important matters."

"They killed each other off."

"Then how do you explain Onnin?"

"I'm afraid, I'm unwilling to relinquish all information."

Royah gave Onnin a questionable look, and he slowly shook his head with puzzlement. Onnin was learning things too, if Melvin could be believed, but he wasn't sure how much he wanted to know.

"He is also the emerger who escaped from my prized experimental arena. Although he is known as a cannibal over the net, he is not. Doesn't deserve the moniker. I know it for a fact. But another fact is that he is something much more brutal."

Onnin's stomach fluttered uncomfortably. "A lie."

"The dead, who you killed with your bare hands, would likely disagree. I examined you over the course of your time inside, as you struggled to survive, wearing goggles capable of seeing at night. My goggles were left over from the war and I found them. They belong to me now. I viewed you and the others from viewpoints I had built encircling the arena."

He felt his anger rise. In ways that was at the precipice of beyond his control.

"Do you remember what it was called? The name of the place? What they called it?"

Of course he remembered. "Yes."

"I paid the greedy emergers for their own people and the experiment allowed me to indulge in a personal curiosity. It showed me

how people would react to such a stressful environment, how they would survive, who would survive, if anyone. It was all answered. I, we, forced evolution, similar to the first humans and their survival on Earth. But within only a few years and not millennia."

Everyone was staring at Onnin now, even Emma, because Royah had twisted in his direction. Their sudden uncertainty about him was no different than how he felt when he was around strangers.

When he was alone, when he seemed to be everyone's enemy while he was hiding, or on the move.

"Though it wasn't the result I anticipated. In a way I was disappointed. I honestly thought you would all work together to find a way out. Not give up and resort to cannibalism."

Onnin nearly objected again, but everything Melvin revealed was objectionable, even if there was some truth. That was his intent. Melvin desired them to fight.

Strangers didn't understand Onnin nor were they interested in taking the time to get to know him, but Royah and Buddy knew him well enough. He considered them friends.

The old man behind the wall was a monster and he was attempting to destroy everything important to him, his real connections with others. Others he cared about. He wasn't about to allow it to happen.

"Afterward, I ceased my research. Possessing all the data I required. I still haven't tracked down the rest. In an exciting way, I enjoy the idea of giving birth to the kind of humans who were capable of such atrocities, willing to do anything to survive, and how the rest of the world would react to them. How many emergers get to do what I did? I hoped to hear of sightings of them over the years, as I did with you, Onnin, but I haven't. They're still out there somewhere. They could be on the other side of Home, for all we know. Experiments often result in many uncertainties. Some of them never end."

Onnin's life was sawed open, a scar already healed but wounded once again. He felt like a young man again. Scared, helpless, angry, and with no control over his life. Especially when he had been cast down into the place so terrible that he didn't want to think of its name.

The conversation was delaying the inevitable. He was going to have to fight his way out. Fight *their* way out.

"Because the radios are open frequency, those on the net speak of you often. You've become something of a favorite person to blather on about, and they naïvely refer to you as a cannibal. Interesting, don't you think?"

As if Onnin would respond to Melvin's deliberate intent to get a rise out of him with only his words.

"The chatterers also like to talk you up as the biggest man on the planet and un-killable, taking shots at you with their guns from across the flat. That you are psychic and know about danger before it happens. Psychic is what some say, but we both know better. It is a battle sense you possess, passed down to you from your ancestors."

They were all really listening to Melvin now, whether they wanted to or not. Though clearly somewhat insane and corrupted by his sense of power, he was revealing much thought-provoking information.

Melvin's speech didn't just anger Onnin, it numbed him too. The revelation about him in the last few minutes was the truth. It was how it was. He knew it. Maybe he always did and needed someone else to say it, before he could accept it.

"I know much about previous human civilizations. What I learned, formed from riddles. They poured all of their knowledge into technology. I'd like to believe that the end result they were hoping for, would result in something unique. New life or artificial life?"

Melvin cleared his throat, sounding even older.

"That was a question to all of you. I see. Not interested in the back and forth you people typically enjoy."

"I've got an answer for you," Buddy countered.

Melvin ignored him. *"I'll go on then. For as much as my own amusement, I suppose. I hardly have anyone to talk to, except for Ash."*

Buddy mouthed something, and Royah shrugged.

If Melvin noticed, he gave no hint. *"At a certain point, whatever is created will replace us. The culmination of knowledge, the pinpoint of what it means to be human, which is freedom of thought and brilliance. Many years ago, we humans were the end result of a culmination. We likely took the place of the dominant life form at the time. We have been the strongest ever since."*

"He's crazy," Buddy whispered.

"I know," Royah whispered back.

"It's happening again. Do you understand? We're doomed. Whatever it is we've become, it will fight us in the realm of every technology we've ever invented. But then again, we've always been doomed, yet we are still here, so we can stop it. We can block our own demise, whether it be by technology or something occurring naturally. We humans are emergers. We direct what is eventual, do you see? The life of this existence, our existence, has chosen to represent itself in the form of a human. Human beings are perfection at a biological level. This is why we're the dominant beings on this planet and others too."

30. ONNIN

"The next evolution *will be even more impressive technology. Each dominant species will advertently or inadvertently replace itself with an even more dominant one. It can occur through evolution or unnaturally, by accident even, and actually inventing the technology evolving to destroy it. That species will reign until the next replaces them."*

Onnin allowed Melvin to go on and on with his hypothetical, hypocritical, redundant, and insane rhetoric. All the while, he was doing his best to figure out a way of escape.

If he couldn't eventually think of something by using his own words to threaten Melvin, he'll charge the wall, break it open, and pull the mad man apart.

"Species is a relative term. I want to push human evolution myself, further than ever before, to preserve humanity and combat the dangers of technology. Though brutal, it is necessary. Merely examine the consequences of Home."

Royah glared at the skinny shadow. "What went wrong?"

"Eventually, the combatants saw everyone as their enemy. They killed women too. Not many people know that. Their own species. How insane they'd become."

"He doesn't know," Buddy said.

"It must be possible that there are more emergers like Onnin?" Royah said to Melvin.

"No."

"I was nothing like my parents," Onnin said.

"He doesn't believe me. But were they your real parents? All of us have lineage to the colonists. Not you, though. Yours is different. Much, much older."

Onnin was taken aback. And also confused. He never thought of it before, but of course he wasn't related to his parents by blood. How could he be? He didn't act like them, or even look like them in any way, including height; he towered over them even as a boy.

They never treated him as a son, even though he wanted them to, more as an inconvenient neighbor child. They were always cold to him. When he was young, he thought it was because of something he'd done but that wasn't why. It was because they weren't related.

Again, something he always suspected deep down but was afraid to acknowledge. Someone like Melvin had told him the truth. Even despicable people were able to enlighten. The truth was also why his parents were able to give him up in Orthal; he wasn't their son.

The knowledge was freeing in a way, but at what point had they accepted him into their lives? And why? Where did he come from? Onnin wasn't about to grovel for more information from the mad man.

Melvin didn't deserve the interest. All he earned was the aim of Onnin's revolver. If only he could find where his gun was hidden. Melvin likely stored their weapons close, considering how confident he was in the confinement of the box.

Onnin would find their belongings and weapons. After he broke them out.

"Now what?" Royah waited without a response. She allowed her frustration to creep in. "Now what, Melvin?"

"Now I get to see what you do."

"See what *who* do?" Buddy said. "What's he talking about?"

Onnin felt intense anger replace what he was feeling moments ago, and rise in strength to such a level he was glad his friends weren't looking at him anymore. It was as if no time passed between then and this trap.

Melvin, it seemed, was responsible for putting him in both terrible places.

Onnin suddenly felt pity for the young man who he'd been,

who was forced to fight his way out. Climb out of where he'd been thrown away. Such horror. Even though he'd practically been a man physically at such a young age, in mind he'd been an innocent.

The place destroyed that innocence, and the person who replaced the young man he was, who fought his way out, was much different.

Melvin made a grave error. Who Onnin became, was conditioned to withstand extreme hardships. To live through the worst savagery his fellow man was capable of. What currently contained him was nowhere near as formidable.

Surviving the place was actually training for the rest of his life, however long it would be, and his present circumstances didn't compare to what he'd been through already. Escaping here would be easier.

"Huh, big guy?" Buddy said, alarm in his voice. "What does he mean, 'what you'll do'?"

"He wants to know which one of you I'll kill first."

Royah reflexively hugged Emma to her chest. "Onnin?"

Onnin went to the wall, causing Melvin to adjust his posture uncomfortably, before speaking into the intercom.

"Did you hear him, Ash? He doesn't deny his brutality. Fascinating. He does remember the Dredge."

Of course Onnin did. The terrible place was a part of him and always would be.

20 Years Ago

31. ONNIN

It was odd, but for the few seconds after he jumped—forced to jump by gunpoint—he felt relief because he was finally out of the rain and suddenly felt warm. The air was hot.

He wasn't sure how he knew what to do, but he rolled as he fell. He hoped not to crush someone by accident.

His speed increased, and he realized what was beneath him, and unable to prevent himself from crushing further what was already long dead.

He kept his mouth shut for fear he would ingest fleshy pieces as he tumbled down the pile, and realized the thuds and smacks he heard while above ground with the armed men, were those who jumped before him connecting with the corpses.

Had they not been there, the others—and maybe even Onnin—either wouldn't have survived the fall or been severely injured. The distance from the opening above to below was at least one hundred feet.

Rolling was his only choice, but also not attempting to brace himself as he flipped, twisted, and turned. Blood smeared over him and he was forced to breathe in the metal stench. He finally tumbled to a stop at the base of the carnage.

There were far too many dead in the pile beneath him to count. He could feel the give. It made him feel sick. It didn't matter how strong he was, nothing could prevent the overwhelming horror of seeing so many lifeless humans.

Before he could stop himself, he retched. The stench of death was overwhelming, far worse than feces, and gag inducing, even after he'd gotten sick. The surrounding decay kept his stomach rolling even though it was empty.

If the entire underground location—depending on how far the bloody ecosystem stretched—was as full of what presently surrounded him, and also beneath him, there could have been thousands of bodies. And there was also the hill of bodies he'd rolled down.

To create a hill of death so high as to break a fall, required more people dying than he wanted to think about. It also meant that they were killed before they were thrown in. It was obvious most died long ago. Why were they cast down? Just to die?

All of it must have been premeditated. It was organized, so there were others who helped plan it besides the armed men above.

Thinking he would no longer retch, he wiped his damp mouth with the back of his hand, noticing that there was blood all over it. But it wasn't his own. While struggling to gain his footing, he somehow tumbled down a slope of even more carnage.

They were mangled, maybe from the fall, and putrid, decomposing guts and entrails looked yanked out. On purpose. After they died, it seemed they were cut open. It frightened him.

Eventually, he made his way to a pool of red wet he dared not drink, even though he was very thirsty, especially after getting sick. He didn't want to think about what the fluid was made of.

The putrid filth would have likely poisoned humans from Earth if ingested, but not those born on Home, not emergers. Emergers were born after the war, the toughest, most resilient human beings ever to live.

They could drink poison. Onnin heard another kid say that at school once. But all humans had similar instincts, whether they were born on Earth or on Home, and ingesting something unknown could be deadly.

There was a booming sound above and when he looked up, the tower of gore was briefly illuminated by lightning, reflecting off the shine of so many bodies and slippery, bloody limbs that it almost looked like a work of art.

Then it was dark again, and he was glad he could no longer see the horrifying spectacle. Would he soon be among the dead too?

Onnin wouldn't just give up and die. He would find a way out. If there was one. There must be. Another problem was that he was immersed in darkness, and now even more so; the men above had dragged something over the opening.

There were around fifty of them and it likely took all their strength. Even if he could climb—surely what he would use to grasp wasn't sturdy—he didn't know if he could push up whatever blocked the hole and then climb out.

It was quieter without the storm above. Just the whimpering of people scattered here and there, in shock, and hiding. He was suddenly aware of the panicked injured, those who did their best to help them, and slushing, stomping, and people running, as if being chased.

It seemed everyone who had jumped had survived because he could hear movements of equally as many, more even, and there were whispers by those trying to decide what to do next.

"It's a sewer."

Onnin didn't recognize the voice. If it was true, at least someone was trying to figure out what the place had been before the war. Knowing might help them escape. But it was strange, he knew. How did he know?

There was a calmness to the way he had spoken. Had he been down here already? Even before the citizens of Orthal?

Onnin was about to ask when everyone went silent, all whispers ceased, and he heard strange movements. It sounded nothing like the other people.

"We should stick together."

It was the same man who had spoken before. He was making himself a leader already, which wasn't always the best idea. Leaders drew attention to themselves. Onnin had learned that while among other kids.

Whoever or whatever was quickly surrounding them did not reply. But weren't they all in the same dire situation?

An abnormal feeling, one Onnin never felt before, washed over him. Similar to how he imagined prey must feel, when being hunted by beasts on Planet Earth. His eyes were adjusting to the darkness quicker than he thought. He spotted mysterious watchers.

They were human, but poised, as if planning to fight. As each second passed, more of them, people who looked like they'd already been cast down, appeared. They'd been here a long time from the looks of them. And they acted expectant.

Human or not, their eyes were predatory, a characteristic Onnin imagined he would see in an animal. They were thin, with long hair, and bushy beards. Every movement was calculated, not wanting to be spotted. Predators on the hunt.

Onnin heard stories about animals from those who read books he'd never read. The way the watchers were behaving, reminded him of what he'd heard. He should tell the others to stay together, as they were now in the territory of outliers.

Except they weren't just outliers; they were underground dwellers, and somehow Onnin knew that made them even more dangerous.

It looked as if one side of the sewer had collapsed in the distance; the ceiling having fallen to the ground. The crumbled opening let in enough dim light to hint at a way out.

It was far off and to reach it would mean climbing over many destroyed obstacles. Including past the beings who threatened. Except no one seemed to have noticed it but himself. Was he the only one who could see it?

His gut told him horrifying things, but reality was a step ahead. He peered past frightened faces to see steadfast ones, eyes suddenly moving in the shadows, and now only feet away.

The place probably took damage during the war. What used to be tunnels, were obliterated by powerful weapons. If there was a way out, then whoever was still here chose to be.

"Now."

The voice was the same who mentioned they were in a sewer and how they should stick together. He was a leader, but not of any of the townsfolk. The hunters converged. It happened so fast.

Shock caused all kinds of effects, Onnin learned. For some, it slowed down time, as it did for himself. For others, it paralyzed them. Their minds couldn't comprehend what was happening. They simply endured the violence.

Onnin reacted as if he'd been through it all before and had trained for it. He had already identified the threats around them. The others seemed oblivious, as if they were blind.

Other than his size—Onnin was able to crouch and hide—he did his best not to stand out in any way, so what was happening to the others wouldn't happen to him. But that, he knew, could change at any second.

He was smart not to align himself with the group. Those he was cast down with, didn't even get the chance to fight back. They barely got the chance to voice their own fright before they were overwhelmed. They were only able to yell in alarm. And scream in pain.

The things who used to be people, were waiting to feed on anything moving. The other corpses already decomposed too much to consume, so live humans were what they hungered for.

The cannibals attacked as any successful predator would, with barely a hint of their presence, movement or sound beforehand.

Onnin was aware of their whereabouts, but the attack happened so fast that even he couldn't warn the others. All he could do was avoid the same fate and hide.

But what if his parents were down here? It was impossible to know. And searching for them would be impossible too. Pointless. He could call out to them, but doing so would be a death sentence. Even for him. He felt guilty. He should be doing more.

But his own survival was all he could think about. He was a young man. A mature one, and big for his age, but there were grown men. They should have to make decisions before him.

In the brief moments that he rationalized his behavior, those who were stalked were grabbed and pinned down. One of them was a woman.

She yelled for someone familiar to help her, Onnin couldn't understand her clearly, but then she screamed for anyone to help her. Louder than he thought possible. It was awful. She was terrified and the high pitch of her pain was amplified in the closeness of the killing.

Someone finally did fight his way over to her, even as all of her was being bitten, but her life was over quickly, so it had been pointless.

Her death distracted, caused an even more sinister panic, and made it easier for the cannibals to identify their prey because they ran. It must have been a plot they'd concocted before. There were far too many of them to be starving.

To be so desperate to eat? And choose human flesh? It was an abominable choice. Onnin was sickened, and could not understand how anyone could choose to live that way. Death would be better.

Whoever became a cannibal, could hardly be considered human. Their minds sick to the point only those who were as vicious, could understand.

He needed to keep his wits about him. He didn't want to die. He was still young. He'd barely lived. He must survive.

Survivors of the initial attack wouldn't be alive much longer. They were panicking and scared and defensive.

Singles separated from the group being eaten, or simply killed to be consumed later, and ran in different directions, trudging through bloody, pooling muck, often tripping over body parts.

Somehow, Onnin was even more invisible, since the present victims drew attention. Like all hunters, and being no different, fleeing prey spurned ferocity.

Who of the cannibals had been potential victims to begin with, but joined who was already down here?

Onnin wasn't sure how long someone could survive considering the gruesome conditions, but since there were so many dead, it was obvious whoever was the strongest. And the most desperate.

In every group, there was always someone who stood out more than the others, a leader, someone smarter or faster or stronger. Onnin knew because he was one of those people.

He also knew, unfortunately, he could survive down here as well. He learned in school that life was a series of choices. Except he would never choose to live as the cannibals did.

Maybe choice had nothing to do with it. He suspected hunger eventually overtook all rational thought. He wondered how long it took for such a transformation. How long would it take before he became like the rest of the monsters?

He was born from the destruction, the poison of the war, as other emergers had been, but what set him apart was his size, strength, and instincts. Somehow, he always knew what to do next during a fight, even when he was younger.

He would never tell anyone because they probably wouldn't understand, or believe him. Yet there it was, inside him somewhere, the real, and because of it, he had the best chance of anyone to survive. And also escape.

Onnin's fight began after stomping in another deep puddle of blood. They didn't try to speak to him or trick him with lies. Aside from the man who spoke, and probably a few others, their communicative ability was too far gone.

They thought of someone, especially someone as big as Onnin, as nothing more than even more meat to consume.

32. ONNIN

A weapon. Some kind of sharp object. It arced in front of him. A miss.

The cannibal slashed again, but Onnin blocked his arm, quickly grasped his wrist, and twisted, knowing either he would go with the roll or his arm would break.

The snapping bone was so loud that it echoed, followed by a shriek of pain. He completely lost interest in Onnin and was instead obsessed with his devastating wound.

The others went after him with their teeth and steaming blood-soaked hands, trying desperately to get a hold of him. Get him off his feet and onto the ground.

There was so much gore everywhere that he had no trouble slipping out of their grasp. But he did struggle to remain upright.

Avoiding so many crazed coming after him, moving quickly, and trying to remain upright was quite the feat, so he fell often. But he always got back up and fast. No choice.

If they cut him open with their weapons—they'd fashioned all kinds of blades meant to cut and slice—or tore him open with their teeth, he would end up as dead as the others.

There was no way to avoid confrontation. He realized what he needed to do: go after the weakest first, and do his best to avoid the ones who held the weapons. But like all plans, none were perfect once executed.

When too many knives were in twice as many hands, he realized he had to change tactics. He made the motion to run, just as the rest who'd made the same mistake, spurning them to chase after him.

But then Onnin turned and went after them, something they

were definitely not expecting. Some ran away. Most did not. They stood their ground defiantly.

Whenever Onnin could get a grip, he grabbed them, threw them into one another, got them on the ground and threw his clenched fists as hard as he could, breaking bones, or crushing skulls. Doing anything to prevent them from moving again.

The glint of their sharp weapons fell out of their hands and sank below the bloody muck.

After the group armed with knives was dead, it gave him the chance to hide for a while. He suspected that it was them who were sent after him first. Hopefully another cannibal wouldn't find the knives.

Now that he understood what he was dealing with, he knew how to fight them. He would kill as many of them as possible and then duck out of view to rest for as long as he could, before being found again.

It was always dark, but he could see better as the days went on. He was getting used to the gloom.

When fighting, it was impossible not to get bit. But then he would know where their mouths were. And then he knew where their rotted minds were located.

Every time they attempted to bite his flesh, he grabbed them by the face and the back of the head and twisted sharply, snapping their necks.

Doing so never prevented the next maniac from attacking the same way, but the more of them he killed, the better chance he had to escape.

Bites hurt, and sometimes stung afterward, but they always healed. He never got sick. It was another example of his resilience.

Some of them grouped together, others alone. One tried a different approach. He actually talked to him, pretending they were friends, and obviously thought Onnin was stupid.

Onnin allowed him to speak, pretending to treat him like any other emerger rather than a creature, until he tried to sink his teeth into his arm. Then Onnin beat him to death.

The faint light grew brighter, the closer he got to it. It was noticeable during—what must be—daytime. Or if the night sky was clear and the moon shone bright.

A full moon was days ago. He hoped he wasn't mistaken and the tiny light was indeed a way out of the nightmare. Real, not a figment of his imagination. Every footstep he took, got him closer to the truth.

Surviving consisted of hiding among bodies, fighting when he must, and moving when none of them was near.

He was wrong about how the others would fare, how he thought they would be killed right away. Some survived the initial attack as he did, but they were far behind him, and over time, they gave themselves away when he did not.

It made him realize that if he was alone, he likely wouldn't have survived. There were too many cannibals, hundreds of them, and the others from Orthal were acting as a diversion for his progression toward the light.

Although he abandoned the people he jumped in with, as the days went on, he didn't feel guilty about it anymore. They were getting themselves—and others—killed because of their impatience, weakness, and fear.

Attempting to save them, any of them, would have meant trying to save all of them. Doing so would have jeopardized his own survival. He didn't know any of them well. He owed them nothing. Down in the Dredge, everyone was on their own.

If his parents had been killed, then he owed everyone else more to escape than fail at saving them. Better he survived, than no one.

Hunger was a problem though. It made him desperate, like those being killed, and those doing the killing, and thirst made hunger worse. He didn't eat, never lowered himself as those who hunted him.

But he was forced to drink what was on the ground, the bloody muck, to survive. At first he thought doing so would poison him because it was so unnatural. Regardless of his shame, the gore kept him alive.

The others were dead already. Even if they—technically—were still alive. They'd probably never make it out of there. As he was going to. He would allow some to follow him if it were possible not to be spotted. But it was unlikely.

The only other survivors would be the cannibals, and he'd gladly leave them behind. They weren't worth saving. Not a one. He didn't care who they'd been before devolving into something south of human. Obvious from the predatory dullness in their eyes.

There seemed to be only one way out. After watching the escape route for days, he noticed it was guarded. Well-guarded.

The cannibals positioned themselves at the outskirts of the shadows, and he watched them act as if the path were open. To encourage attempts. It would allow their prey easier to overwhelm. Others obviously had attempted what he was about to do but failed.

He would not fail. It was time to make a move.

Being cast down, he had been regarded as nothing but a piece of meat to feed mindless monsters. But that had transformed anger into strength, causing something within him to switch to a survival mode, a notch so low in himself he hadn't even known it was there.

His motion alerted them. Onnin wasn't trying to hide anymore. He was ready for the final fight. Wanted it even, so he yelled. He didn't recognize his own voice. He didn't sound like himself, as he became as vicious as his enemies.

They rushed him even though they were afraid. He saw it when they were close. At first, it was one at a time who tried to take him down, probably their strongest, but when they realized one against him was impossible, numbers grew to five or six.

Once over a dozen, but their ends were the same; beaten to death and him moving toward freedom.

They, like himself, lived through every poison and infection that could kill a person on Home, so in one respect they were his equal.

Except they weren't as strong, and he was only down there for days, not however long it took to transform humans into monsters. The drive to live gave him more strength than a full stomach ever could.

Trudging forward, he ended lives, and with every footstep he became a fiercer killer. Fewer arcing ragged blades slashed. He caught arms with ease and snapped them.

He beat his fists into the face of anyone who tried to grab or bite him, and struck them until they were still. He made sure they were dead, giving them extra punches to the head until skulls burst or crushed inward.

To those observing—not fighting—it must have looked like a wrestling match, except it was dozens against Onnin. They rushed him crazily, without skill or forethought, and he knocked them to the ground and threw them into one another.

He broke arms.

Demolished faces.

Stomped on legs to break them at sensitive places, causing howls of pain.

He even picked a man over his head to bring him down over his knee, breaking his back.

They didn't speak to him anymore, not a one. They grunted and yelled, their wild eyes displaying their inability to produce rational thoughts. They were more like animals than men. No reasoning with them.

They were insane, how could they not be, and language was not useful in a pit of slaughter.

Onnin was big, but still a young man, almost a man but not. They were adults, driven insane by hunger and corrupted by solitude and the disappearance of the world they once knew.

During their final moments, they learned who Onnin truly was; a killer far worse than anyone they'd ever encountered before.

If they knew what he was capable of, they probably would have allowed him to leave. But maybe some part of them wanted to be put out of their misery.

This was no place for humans, surely fragmented memories

still resided somewhere inside their rotted minds.

They anticipated what he was about to do. A challenge to their control. They were being disrespected, and because no one had escaped so far, they made one final attempt to converge on him.

They likely believed that by all grouping together and winning this fight, it would give them free reign to hunt. It was probably true because they wouldn't encounter a threat like him for the rest of their lives.

His impatience got the better of him and he hurried, he was so close now, the warmth of the light practically within reach.

There was a ledge tilted up at the ceiling. Fallen down at the right angle for him to climb onto.

But he tripped, and many of the bloodthirsty killers climbed on top of him, doing their best to overwhelm him as they had the others.

When they grasped at his powerful arms, he punched and kicked, threw them down or picked them up to crush them against any dilapidated or crumbling surface nearby.

Getting to his feet, he yelled like some great giant, angrily throwing them away and sending them tumbling.

He broke the arms of those who somehow still gripped his clothing, stomped on one of their hands when they wouldn't let go, and then stomped on as many heads, causing them to burst.

A punch was thrown in slow motion. Onnin tapped it away. The thrower was unconscious the moment Onnin drove his fist into his face, and then dead as his face caved in. Teeth sunk into his calf and Onnin yelled.

He looked down to see an animal of a man with no hint of human in his eyes. Instead, there was a different and wicked intelligence that had been born in this place. He was missing part of his nose and both his ears.

The thing, who used to be a man, tore out a chunk of Onnin's calf flesh with his teeth, causing him to grimace. Though the thing's nose was chewed off, raw and exposed, Onnin kicked him there anyway.

The recent biter disappeared within the desperate group of

more clawing for him. The cannibals were growing in number right before his eyes. It was as if the dead surrounding him rose up to join enemy ranks.

Strength Onnin didn't know was possible, was used to kill the enemies trying to block him from the rest of his life.

He hoped to use what was happening, as a further transformation to help him survive battles yet to come. Once he left the nightmare.

Onnin's life had been about fighting so far. No reason to believe it would end. He trudged upward, climbing, kicking, yelling.

The glow he killed toward wasn't day, it was night, but to him night was as bright as the sun. Darkness had been the light of his existence.

He felt wind, a welcome cold, and then raindrops. A storm, just as there'd been when he was abducted from Orthal.

Sharp ends jutted out of the structure and cut him as he crawled his way through openings too small but he didn't care.

Felt steel and cement move away, kicked at enemies beneath him still trying to grab hold of his feet and drag him back down below.

He was colder but felt better the higher he climbed, the cool splash of rain curtains drenched him, the wet transforming to steam as it met the heat of his body.

Finally, Onnin sturdied himself on soft mud instead of bloody carnage.

The next foot found the sturdiness of open ground. The flat.

The storm washed the dark gore off him in thick rivers of filth. He caught his breath, exhausted, and turned, watching the hole.

But no more hands reached for him out of the darkness. Tearing his view away from it to gaze out into the night, he saw no other threats.

A man, a warrior, marched away from the Dredge, leaving the innocent young man he'd been within its violent depths.

www.ingramcontent.com/pod-product-compliance
Lightning Source LLC
LaVergne TN
LVHW050548160826
845677LV00011B/2231

* 9 7 9 8 7 3 0 8 9 0 9 8 5 *